Dylan Stone and Serena Fields have been best of friends their entire lives. For Dylan, she's the solid, dependable woman in his life. His person. The one who has been there for him through the best and worst of times and doesn't see him for the millions he has in the bank. And even though he's been secretly attracted to her for years, there are some lines that best friends don't cross—even if he does spend most of their time together entertaining dirty thoughts about her that have no business being in his head.

Serena has been in love with Dylan Stone for as long as she can remember, but she's searching for her happily-ever-after and that's not her best friend's thing. Unfortunately, her dating life is one disaster after another, yet Dylan is always there with a pint of her favorite ice cream and a listening ear after each and every disappointing encounter.

It's the perfect arrangement, until one night changes everything.

Chapter One

THE LAST THING Dylan Stone expected at nine-fifteen on Friday evening was a knock on his door. He was equally surprised to find his best friend, Serena Fields, standing on the other side of the threshold, considering it was supposed to be the night that she'd intended to go all the way and seal the deal with her latest guy after holding out on him for the past five weeks.

She'd definitely dressed to impress and seduce her date. The sexy little red number she'd chosen to wear for the occasion molded to her curves like a second skin from chest to thighs, and it was all Dylan could do to keep his gaze from lowering to the upper swells of her breasts being pushed up by the tight, strapless band of fabric wrapped around her tempting body.

Don't fucking look, he told himself, because ogling his best friend's full, lush tits wasn't cool. And because he'd spent years keeping his attraction to her a secret from everyone around him, and especially from her, he

1

managed to maintain that normal outward indifference to Serena as a desirable woman, despite the heated lust coursing through his veins. If she'd been any other female, he would have already had that fuck-me dress on the floor and his cock buried eight inches deep inside her.

Surprisingly, it was those dirty thoughts that made him aware of the fact that nothing about her appearance announced that her latest Mr. Right had enjoyed what she'd been offering. There were no wrinkles in her dress, her makeup wasn't smudged, and her honey-blonde hair looked impeccably styled and untouched by a man's hands—unless her date was one of those self-centered guys who had no clue how to please a woman in the bedroom.

Then he recognized the disappointment in her blue eyes and the discouraged slump of her bare shoulders. He was all too familiar with that look of utter defeat because he'd seen it dozens of times before. It told him that yet another douchebag had shattered those hopes and dreams she harbored of finding a husband, getting married, and having babies.

"I take it things didn't go well with Dick?" he asked, stepping back and opening the door wider for her to come in.

"No, it didn't go well at all, and his name is Darren," she corrected as she passed by Dylan, enveloping his senses in a soft, seductive perfume that made his lower region stir inappropriately.

"Darren . . . Dick." He shrugged unapologetically as he closed the door and followed her into his living room, doing his best to keep his eyes off her swaying ass. "Close enough."

She turned around to face him, the barest hint of a smile on her red, glossy lips at the nickname he'd given the latest guy who'd crushed all her expectations and had hurt his best girl. His attempt at humor in these situations—and there had been way too many of them—always helped to lighten the moment, and her mood. He was the guy who was always there to pick up the pieces of her fractured confidence, who bolstered her esteem and encouraged her to give dating a new guy another try. That's what best friends did, because she deserved a good man in her life and that fairy-tale ending she'd been chasing for years.

Her smile faltered as her gaze took in his naked chest, the old, worn sweatpants riding low on his hips, then back up to the hair he knew was all over the place because he'd run his fingers through it a few times while figuring out the glitch in one of the newest apps he was building.

Ironically enough, Serena's dating woes had inspired The Boyfriend Experience app he was currently working the bugs out of, which offered a woman the ability to choose the perfect man for her based on her ideals and qualifications—mostly for a temporary arrangement when they needed a quick, on-the-spot fake boyfriend for an event or other occasion. But this latest issue in the code was frustrating the hell out of him and putting him behind on launching the app.

"Umm, I didn't catch you at a bad time, did I?" she asked, her voice dropping a husky octave as her pretty blue eyes darted around the room, clearly looking for evidence that he had a guest over.

"If you're asking if I have a woman here, no, I don't." Not that it would matter. He'd always put Serena first, before any female he brought home for the evening. Which was all those dates ever were— casual, no strings, and usually one-night stands because emotional ties were so not his thing. "I was just working on the Boyfriend Experience app and trying to figure out where the problem is in the interface. You know, nerd stuff," he teased.

Her expression softened with relief that he was alone, and she tossed her small purse on a chair in the living room and returned her gaze to his. "Good, because I really need to vent about my awful night. But first, this tight dress that I can barely breathe in and these stupid shoes that are killing my feet are coming off."

With that announcement, she whirled around and

headed down the hallway to his master bedroom, making herself right at home like she always did. As soon as he heard her rifling through his dresser drawers, he headed into the kitchen to get phase two of her breakup routine started. He opened the side-by-side freezer and reached for the only thing that helped to cure her dating-night blues . . . a pint of Ben and Jerry's Chocolate Fudge Brownie ice cream.

It wasn't a coincidence that he always had at least three cartons of the flavor on hand at all times. He was always prepared for a late-night visit, because inevitably, Serena's idiotic dates fucked up a good thing and she ended up on his doorstep to wallow in her inability to find a decent, honorable man—one who didn't come with any kind of obnoxious traits, offensive mannerisms, or disturbing personal issues that slowly, eventually, made themselves known over their time together.

He couldn't wait to hear what this latest moron had done to let such an amazing woman slip through his fingers, he thought with a smirk. Especially on a night that should have ended in hot, sweaty, multiple-orgasm sex. What guy in his right mind screwed up that kind of sure thing?

Dylan grabbed a spoon from the drawer and frowned at the unwelcome image that filled his head of another dude getting it on with his best girl friend.

Okay, if he was honest with himself, Dylan had to admit that he was grateful that the night had been aborted, because he hated knowing or hearing about some other man kissing her, touching her, and doing all the dirty things he'd spent years privately fantasizing about doing with and to Serena.

And how awful was it that he could breathe a little easier when these guys did something stupid or didn't live up to Serena's standards, and she ended things with them? Not because he enjoyed seeing her upset or hurt, but if he was truly honest with himself, he was dreading the day when someone else came along and replaced him in her life as her best friend. It was inevitable that it would happen at some point, and he didn't like thinking about the possibility.

With her carton of ice cream in hand, he headed into the living room and settled on his dark gray sectional couch, comprised of a large sofa and a chaise lounge attached at the end where he sat. Then onto phase three . . . turning on the Hallmark Channel on the TV so it was playing in the background for now. A few years ago, he'd subscribed to the on-demand service just for her because she loved watching the sentimental movies that gave her hope for the next guy, while he endured the eye-rolling, corny shows for her sake and tried to keep his snarky comments to a minimum while she swooned over the predictable romantic plot.

Down the hall, where the guest bathroom was located, he could hear Serena moving around and water splashing in the sink, then a few minutes later she returned, her now bare feet padding softly on the hardwood floor. He wasn't surprised to see that she'd washed her face free of the makeup she'd worn for her date, or the fact that she was wearing one of his old T-shirts, despite having a dedicated drawer and closet space in the guest bedroom, where she kept spare clothes for these impromptu sleepovers.

And yes, he already knew she was staying the night . . . because it was a Friday evening and once her stomach was full of her creamy dessert and she'd finished raking her latest dating disaster over the coals, she'd eventually fall asleep on his couch while they watched one of the latest Hallmark movies. And when she woke up in the morning, she'd expect him to make her the chocolate chip pancakes she loved. It was a ritual they'd done dozens of times before.

He sank into the corner of the couch and stretched his arms across the back cushions, knowing he was probably going to hell for noticing the gentle bounce of her breasts beneath his shirt and the outline of her puckered nipples grazing the soft cotton as she approached. The shirt ended mid-thigh, and instead of taking a long, leisurely journey down her gorgeous legs, he commended himself for lifting his gaze back to her freshly scrubbed face.

But Jesus Christ, there was something so fucking sexy about a woman wearing a man's shirt—specifically, *his shirt*—and little else, though Serena was the only female he'd ever allowed that privilege. The first time she'd changed into one of his shirts their freshman year of high school, she'd explained that she liked how the material smelled like him, and being wrapped in his scent made her feel safe and secure.

What she didn't realize was, by the time she left in the morning and returned his shirt after sleeping in it all night long, it was *her* fragrance that lingered on the fabric. More times than not, he found himself reduced to his horny, fourteen-year-old self as he buried his nose in the material, inhaled her soft, powdery scent, and imagined the hand stroking his aching cock was hers, instead of his own. It was his one guilty pleasure, since those moments were the closest he'd ever get to satiating his desire for her.

With a heavy sigh, she plopped down onto the couch cushion next to him, causing her breasts to jiggle temptingly once again. She crossed her legs in front of her and tucked the hem of his shirt in between her thighs, but not before unknowingly giving him a quick, memorable glimpse of the red lace panties she'd worn to seduce her dipshit of a date.

After reaching for the pint of Ben and Jerry's he'd set on the coffee table, Dylan pulled off the lid and handed her the carton, along with the spoon.

"Thank you," she murmured, and dived right in to the ice cream.

He gave her a couple of minutes to enjoy a few bites and get all that chocolatey goodness into her bloodstream. When he could no longer handle her soft, husky moans of pleasure as she indulged in the treat, as if mere ice cream could make up for the fact that she'd been denied the orgasm she'd been hoping for tonight, he decided it was time to find out why she'd ended up at his place instead of in her date's bed.

"So, what happened with Dick? You've been dating him for five weeks now, so I can't imagine what went wrong . . . unless he's gay or likes to dress up in women's lingerie?" he joked.

She shook her head, her lips pursing seriously. "No. Worse than that."

He raised his brows at her dismayed tone. "Jesus. What could be worse than either of those scenarios?"

Her brows furrowed even more as she met his gaze, her own troubled. "He's thirty-seven years old, he's a finance manager for a car dealership, and money doesn't seem to be an issue for him, considering how he dresses and what he spends on our dates," she said.

"Okaaay," Dylan replied, unable to find fault in

any of those things.

"He drives a brand-new Mercedes," she went on, waving her spoon in the air, her gestures and tone growing agitated. "He sends me a dozen roses every week at work and wants to take me to Fiji on vacation."

Dylan scratched a finger against his temple in complete and utter confusion. The guy sounded damn near perfect. "So flowers and romantic getaways are suddenly a deal breaker for you?"

"No," she said, adorably exasperated with *him* now. "Darren is almost forty, and he's portrayed himself as a successful, financially stable guy, but tonight, I find out that he *lives in his mother's basement.*"

"Maybe it's just a temporary arrangement?" he suggested, trying to give the other guy the benefit of the doubt.

Serena shook her head as her lush, pink lips removed another dollop of ice cream from her spoon. "No, it's not an interim thing, because I flat out asked. He's never moved out of the house he's lived in since childhood with his mother, and doesn't plan to."

Dylan blanched in disbelief and had to admit that the scenario was the stuff that horror stories were made of. "Okay, that's creepy as fuck."

"I know, right?" she said, sounding vindicated that he agreed with her. "That's what I thought when I realized he lived in a basement! I could hear his mother moving around upstairs when we first entered the place through a back entrance. And then, as if she'd been waiting for Darren to get home, she opened the basement door, called down to him, and asked if he and his date wanted a slice of Darren's favorite chocolate cake she'd made."

As Serena explained the comical situation, Dylan started to chuckle, and by the time she finished, he was in stitches and laughing so hard he snorted.

She grabbed one of the throw pillows on the couch and smacked him in the face with it. "It's not funny!" she said indignantly, because she always took these dates very seriously, mainly because she was looking for that forever guy and they always disappointed, one way or another.

He pressed a hand to his aching side, still laughing. "No, it's fucking *hilarious*."

"You're such a jerk," she said, though the corner of her mouth twitched with humor, which was exactly what he wanted. Darren the Dick wasn't worth her frustration or anger.

"How did you not know this about him before tonight?" Dylan asked, more serious now. "You've been dating him for five weeks."

"Don't remind me, because I'm feeling incredibly stupid for investing that kind of time in him," she said with a shake of her head. "I honestly thought he was just being a gentleman about sleeping with me and not pressuring me by taking me to his place."

Dylan clearly remembered the day that Serena had met Darren, because he'd gone to the car lot with her when she'd traded her small, fuel-efficient vehicle for a newer model and had witnessed the flirtatious overtures between the two of them once Darren discovered that Serena was single and Dylan was just a friend. By the time she'd signed the finance paperwork and had her new keys in hand, the other guy had Serena's digits in his phone with a promise to call and set up a date.

Up until this point, Darren had practically checked all the pertinent boxes as the prince charming Serena had been searching for. Economically stable, *check*. Attentive and thoughtful, *check*. Emotionally available, *check*. Hell, they'd also talked about the fact that they both wanted marriage and a family.

Even the few times that Dylan had been around him, he'd never seen a cause for concern, which maybe, in hindsight, should have been a cause for concern, he thought wryly. No guy was without their issues and faults . . . especially one who was thirty-seven and had never been married. Obviously, there was a reason for that, and tonight Serena had discovered her date's fatal flaw that had undoubtedly ended many relationships before theirs ... the fact that Darren was first and foremost a mama's boy and probably always would be.

She put her half-eaten carton of ice cream on the coffee table and exhaled a huge sigh. "I guess I should have suspected something wasn't right since we always went to my apartment after a date because he claimed it was easier or closer or some other reason that I accepted. And tonight, being the *big night*," she said, putting the two words in air quotes, "he wanted to take me to a nice hotel and spend the night there, but that just felt ... well, cheap to me. Especially for our first time together. So, I suggested we go to his place, and while I know he wasn't thrilled with the idea, I told him that it was important to me to see where he lived."

"Surprise!" Dylan said facetiously.

"No kidding," she said, then lifted her chin in that stubborn way Dylan knew oh so well. "At first, I thought maybe he lived at home because his mother was sick or something, but that didn't seem to be the case. When I expressed my concern about his living arrangements with his mother, when I need a man who is self-sufficient rather than codependent on a parent at thirty-seven years old, he had the nerve to get defensive and mad at me for being insensitive!"

Yeah, Dylan wasn't shocked that didn't go over

well.

"And *then*, he informed me that he *had* to live with his mother, because he was so far in debt that he couldn't afford a place of his own," Serena said, her disappointment etched all over her face.

Dylan groaned, knowing that revelation had definitely sealed the other man's fate. Serena had grown up with a mother who spent money frivolously, to the detriment of barely being able to make rent, pay utilities, and care for her two daughters after Serena's father had passed away. Since then, Nina had already married and divorced five men, who were all flash and no substance, mostly because she liked being a kept woman.

Unfortunately, Serena's younger sister, Christie, had followed in her mother's footsteps, whereas for Serena, her childhood experiences and Nina's behavior made her more determined not to make the same mistakes. As a result, Serena was practical, responsible, and independent . . . and not so patiently waiting for her Mr. Right to come along and give her the things she desired the most. Stability. Security. Love, commitment, and a family.

He reached out and placed his hand on her knee, giving it an understanding squeeze while trying not to think about how soft her skin felt against the pads of his fingers, or how badly he wanted to trail those same fingers up the inside of her smooth, supple thigh . . .

Swallowing hard, he forcibly banished the direction of those thoughts from his mind before his body followed suit. "Look, the way I see things, you dodged a major bullet," Dylan told her, trying to soften the blow.

She made an annoyed sound beneath her breath and muttered, "How many bullets do I have to dodge before I find a guy who isn't a jerk and treats me like I'm important to him or doesn't disappoint me in some way? Or one who isn't a cheat or has a wandering eye? And then there've been the men who aren't looking for anything more than just a fuck buddy, or think women need to cater to their every whim like a '50s housewife."

He blinked at her and deadpanned, "I don't know why that last point is such an issue for you. That's my number one prerequisite when it comes to dating a woman. You know, it's all about me and what *I* need." He grinned.

She rolled her eyes, but a smile threatened to appear on her lips, too. "You're such a liar, and your sweet but fierce mother would strip your hide if she heard you talking like that."

"True." He chuckled as he kicked his feet up onto the chaise part of the couch so he could stretch out more comfortably. His mother had raised her three sons to be gentlemen, respectful of women, and to treat them as their equal. Anything less and, yeah, he'd be in a world of hurt.

Serena grabbed the pillow she'd hit him with earlier, settled it in her lap, and absently played with the fringe around the edges. "*Your* problem is, you've been a commitment-phobe most of your life, and especially since your breakup with Brandy," she said, reminding him why he kept his own relationships casual and short term, because for the long haul, women demanded and expected more from him than he was able to give.

"And don't forget all the other women who find out I have money and see me as their sugar daddy," he added for good measure.

Truthfully, he hadn't always been stupid wealthy, and having millions had never been his goal, but his company, Stone Media, had catapulted him into a seven-figure-a-year income over the past two years, all because he got paid for what he loved to do—creating and designing apps. For himself. And for big-name companies. Having more money in the bank than he personally needed had just been a bonus.

"You know, not all women are money grubbers like the ones you've come across lately," she said gently.

He tipped his head to the side and arched a brow.

"And not all men are like the ones *you've* dated," he retorted wryly.

She laughed lightly, but the sound was tinged with a bit of sadness. "I don't know that I believe you."

"Touché, sweetheart." Because he didn't believe what she'd just said about the women he'd attracted lately. After Brandy had blindsided him, trust didn't come nearly as easily as it once had. And even before her, that trust had been precarious at best.

Shaking her head at his rejoinder, Serena placed the throw pillow on his thighs, scooted around on the sofa, then laid her head in his lap, making herself comfortable as she stared up at the ceiling and contemplated life. As he looked down at her, there was a furrow between her brows he wanted to smooth away with his fingers, but he refrained from touching her so intimately. It was hard enough—pun intended—that her silky, honey-blonde hair was tumbled across his bare stomach so sensually, so temptingly, and conjured arousing images that had no business being in his brain.

After a few quiet moments, she spoke again. "So much for having a date to Leo and Peyton's wedding next month," she said of his brother's nuptials. "I really thought Darren might be the one."

She sounded so dejected. "He doesn't deserve you," he replied, meaning it. Dylan hated that she couldn't find a decent guy, and it wasn't for a lack of trying. Serena had been on a mission to find "the one" since graduating from college, which added up to five years of dating and disappointments.

Her gaze shifted from the ceiling to his face, her big, blue, emotion-filled eyes meeting his. "Why can't I find someone like you?" she whispered.

Her comment was like a punch to his gut, and Dylan struggled to breathe, because he knew she was being completely serious in her wish. Hell, she might as well have said, *I want it to be you*, since those words were more accurate and truthful.

Dylan wasn't the obtuse idiot everyone thought he was when it came to the beautiful, smart, sexy woman who'd been his best friend since they'd both been in diapers. Despite pretending as though he couldn't see that Serena had worn her heart on her sleeve for years when it came to him, and that he wasn't aware of the longing way she occasionally looked at him—*like now*—he'd always known exactly how she felt about him. That she was *in* love with him.

He cared for Serena. Would do anything for her, and yes, he loved her because she was his best friend. His rock. His other half. His desire and attraction to her weren't part of the equation when it came to his feelings for Serena, because he'd never act on those urges and risk ruining their friendship, since he'd never be able to give her the things she longed for the most.

And the truth was, he'd never been *in* love. Not even with Brandy. He didn't trust that intense level of intimacy that meant being open and vulnerable, which was why he'd always avoided that kind of emotional depth and commitment to one person. He supposed it didn't help his frame of mind that his father had set a shitty example of just how much someone could hurt the person they'd committed their life to, claimed to love, yet could so easily walk away from his wife and family while Dylan's mother was battling breast cancer. Those painful years had made him more self-contained with his emotions, including not putting his heart on the line.

So, no, he wasn't the forever guy Serena was searching for. She deserved so much better than him, a man who had no clue how to love in the capacity she needed. And ultimately, he wanted that for her.

It was that thought that prompted his teasing reply. "I'm hardly a great catch and have my own commitment issues, as you just so kindly pointed out."

Smiling up at him, she lifted her hand and pressed her cool palm against his cheek. "Yeah, but at least I'd know what I was getting with you."

It was difficult seeing the yearning in her eyes and not being able to give this woman everything she wanted and desired. "Trust me, sweetheart, there's a guy out there for you."

But that man wasn't him, no matter how badly she might want it to be.

Chapter Two

"MISS FIELDS, ROBBIE keeps yanking on my hair and it hurts," Annaleise, one of Serena's third-grade students, complained from her desk in the middle of the classroom. "Tell him to stop."

Serena glanced up from the spelling papers she was grading, not surprised that the eight-year-old boy sitting behind Annaleise, who was supposed to be reading quietly, had a guilty look plastered on his face. It also didn't help that he was looking toward the front of the room like a deer caught in headlights—a very guilty deer at that.

"Robbie, please stop pulling on Annaleise's braid and keep your hands to yourself, or I'm going to have to move you up front," Serena said calmly, giving the little boy his one and only warning.

"Yes, ma'am," he replied solemnly, his face a bright pink at now being the center of unwanted attention.

Serena didn't miss the small, satisfied look on Annaleise's face as they both picked up their chapter books and continued to silently read along with the rest of the class. With it being well into the second semester of the school year, Serena knew all of her students well enough to distinguish each child's personality. Robbie wasn't a bully. He just had a little boy crush on Annaleise, and it didn't help matters that the little girl sometimes encouraged the attention and at other times tattled on him, like today.

Serena hid a smile as she returned to grading the papers in front of her. Annaleise and Robbie reminded her a great deal of her and Dylan at that age. Mostly mischievous and playful, but there had been moments of antagonizing one another, as well. They'd squabbled like best friends did, but always resolved their differences.

It wasn't until their freshman year in high school that their friendship started to change, and Dylan was more careful with what had once been innocent flirtations and touches between them. Instead, she'd watched him use that Stone family charm and those panty-dropping dimpled smiles on other girls and keep his interaction with her strictly platonic. That had been her first real introduction to envy and jealousy, because she'd hated watching him with those other girls.

She'd always hoped that he'd see her as more than just his best girl friend, but it never happened. While she'd secretly yearned for him, he'd enjoyed all the perks and female flattery his gorgeous good looks had afforded him . . . until one day, the carefree life as he'd known it had come crashing down around him, and the close-knit, loving family he'd taken for granted had splintered apart at the seams.

The first shock had been the day his mother had been diagnosed with stage-two breast cancer . . . followed shortly thereafter by his father's affair with a woman fifteen years younger than him coming to light. Instead of choosing to stick by the woman he'd married when she needed him the most and being there for the sons they were raising together, Dylan's father asked for a divorce because the woman he was screwing around with was pregnant.

Serena clearly remembered how devastated and angry Dylan had been when it all happened. While Serena had grown up without a father and was used to a selfish mother who hadn't made her daughters a priority because she'd been more concerned about finding her next meal ticket, that hadn't been the case for Dylan. Up until that point in his life, he'd believed that his family was solid as a rock, and his father's actions and choices had changed him from the happy-go-lucky boy he'd been into a man who was a bit jaded, cautious when it came to relationships, and guarded with his emotions.

He was a man who didn't believe in happily-ever-afters—as he'd made clear on more than one occasion, and most recently the night of the Darren fiasco during that vulnerable moment when she'd asked Dylan why she couldn't find someone like him. No, marriage and kids weren't on his radar at all, and Serena refused to settle for anything less than the total package. Even if she was growing weary of all the years she'd spent dating dozens of Mr. Wrongs.

The recess bell rang just as Chelsea, her friend and a part-time substitute teacher at the school, stepped into her class. Serena stood up from her desk as her students quietly but quickly formed a single line by the back door in the room that led to the playground, each child knowing that their good behavior and following the rules Serena had set the first week of school would give them their ticket to fifteen minutes of freedom. Any tussles, arguments, or rambunctious antics, and they'd spend their recess sitting at their desks writing an essay instead.

Serena was always relieved when they behaved, because she needed the break just as much as they did, and today they were perfect little angels. She opened the metal door, and once they were outside, they scattered in different directions. The last thing she heard as the door was closing was Annaleise, who was with two other girls, turn to Robbie and say, "Let's play tag and you're it!", which prompted the little boy to chase after her, just as she wanted.

Clearly, Annaleise was already mastering the art of playing hard to get.

"You run a tight ship in this classroom, Miss Fields," Chelsea teased, leaning a hip against Serena's desk.

Serena shrugged as she walked to the whiteboard spanning the wall behind her desk. "I love kids, but chaos doesn't work for me, and I've learned that if I set down rules and have consequences, nine times out of ten I get law and order from my students. It's that simple."

Chelsea turned where she was perched to keep Serena in her view. "Some of the other teachers could learn a thing or two from you."

"We all have our own way of doing things." Picking up the dry eraser, she swiped it over the glossy whiteboard, erasing that morning's lesson on the differences between action verbs, linking verbs, and helping verbs. "How's Mr. Snyder's class behaving for you today while he's gone?"

"Not nearly as well as yours," she said with a laugh. "Sixth graders are such a pain in the ass."

Serena grinned over her shoulder at her friend as she picked up a black marker and uncapped the tip. "Yeah, at that age they're harder to train because all those hormones are starting to kick into gear. Mood swings, estrogen and testosterone in the air, bodies changing, and fun rebellious attitudes to deal with. Good times."

"And that's why I'm a substitute teacher," Chelsea said with humor as Serena wrote today's math equations on the board for her class to do after recess. "I move on before they truly get on my nerves."

Serena much preferred having one class for a year with the same students. Because despite the occasional pandemonium, she enjoyed bonding with her kids. She liked being that stable influence in their lives and someone they could trust.

"So, what are you doing on Saturday?" Chelsea asked her.

Serena thought ahead to her weekend calendar, which was woefully empty, except for the laundry and grocery shopping she needed to get done. "Not much. What's up?"

"Well, Ava and I are having a small get-together with friends. Just an afternoon barbeque at our place, and it's completely casual," she said of herself and her other friend and roommate. "Aaaand, there might be a guy there that I think you'd hit it off with really well."

Serena abruptly stopped writing on the board and turned to face her friend. "Are you setting me up on a blind date?" she asked incredulously.

She gave Serena an impish grin. "Maybe?" Laughter infused her voice.

"You're kidding me, right?" Chelsea knew how badly things had ended with Darren, which was only three weeks ago. And even though she wasn't nursing a broken heart over the breakup, she dreaded the thought of starting the entire getting-to-know-you ritual all over again. God, she was a serial dater and hated it.

"You gotta get back in the saddle at some point."

Finished with the math problems, she recapped her marker and set it on her desk, her gaze now on her friend. "Is that saddle reference any indication of his personality?" she asked, only half joking. "Like, are we dealing with a donkey? A.k.a. an ass?"

Chelsea cracked up. "Not that I'm aware of."

"How do *you* know him?" Serena asked, crossing her arms over her chest. Yes, she was interrogating her friend. That's how skittish she'd become of being "set up" with a "great guy."

"I don't know him personally," she admitted. "He works as a pharmaceutical rep with Ava, but in a different division. But she's assured me that he's legitimate."

"Legitimate?" Serena repeated, her tone skeptical. "What does that even mean?"

"It means he has his shit together. Ashton is in his

early thirties, has a stable, great-paying job, and he just bought his own place, which already makes him a better catch than Darren." She grinned.

Serena still wasn't convinced. If the guy was such a catch, then why was he still single? Ugh. See, this was what she'd been reduced to . . . being cynical about men. But she knew her judgment of Ashton wasn't fair, because the same could be said for her. She'd like to think that she had a lot of favorable qualities to offer a man, but *she* was still unmarried, as well, with a long list of terminated relationships to her credit. So, really, who was she to be a critic?

The recess bell rang, indicating that break time was nearly over. Within a few minutes, her kids would be lined up outside the classroom and hopefully ready to focus on math for the next forty minutes.

"Quit overthinking things, Serena," Chelsea said, trying to diffuse her hesitation. "It's not an actual date and there's no pressure. You're just meeting Ashton at a casual barbeque, and if the two of you hit it off, great. If not, no big deal."

And maybe, if she was really lucky, she'd have a date to take with her to Leo and Peyton's upcoming wedding. "Fine. Okay," she finally relented as she headed for the back door to let in her class. "I'll go to your barbeque this weekend and meet Ashton."

And hoped she didn't end up regretting her decision.

Chapter Three

"TWO DOWN, ONE to go," Aiden, Dylan's oldest sibling, said with a too jovial slap on Dylan's back. "Your turn is next, little brother."

Dylan refrained, just barely, from rolling his eyes at Aiden, who was deliriously, happily married and now believed both of his brothers needed to be experiencing the same marital bliss, as well. Before his wife, Daisy, had come along, Aiden had been just as guarded and skeptical about committing himself to one woman, so it was almost amusing that he was now championing the union of marriage.

The same could be said for Dylan's other brother, Leo, who'd once been stood up at the altar and had experienced his share of heartbreak, yet had managed to somehow give love another try with Peyton. Today the two of them were getting hitched in Peyton's parents' backyard in a small outdoor ceremony and reception, so of course, love was in the air, and Aiden apparently thought it was important to remind Dylan that he, too, could find the love of his life.

"I'm one hundred percent happy living life as a bachelor," he told his older brother, because it was true for the most part. "I've got a great job that I love, I come and go as I please, and since you've produced a grandchild for mom to dote on, I'm off the hook for that, too."

At the mention of Aiden's kid, Dylan followed his brother's gaze as he glanced at his wife, Daisy, who was standing a few feet away with their mother, Grace, and her boyfriend, Charles, as the trio entertained the admittedly adorable baby in Daisy's arms with tickles and exaggerated baby talk conversation. At six months old, little Isabella Stone was all big blue eyes and chubby cheeks, with a gregarious personality that even Dylan found irresistible.

Aiden pushed back the sides of his suit jacket and slid his hands into his slacks pockets, a ridiculously sappy smile on his face. "Daisy is the best thing to ever happen to me, and that little girl has completely stolen my heart in ways I didn't even think possible."

Yeah, his brother was completely and totally whipped by the two ladies in his life. "I agree, she is kinda cute. Isabella, I mean," he clarified, deliberately alluding to a private joke between them, the one that reminded Aiden that Dylan had almost asked Daisy out on a date before he'd known that his brother had already knocked her up. Yeah . . . talk about awkward.

"Ha, ha," Aiden said in a droll tone. "Very funny."

Dylan pulled his cell phone from his pocket to check the time, then glanced around the backyard. In fifteen minutes, they all needed to take their seats for the ceremony, and Serena had yet to arrive with her date . . . Asher or Ashby or Ashley or some other pretentious name like that. It was Serena's second official outing with the guy she'd been introduced to by her friend, Chelsea, and when he'd texted Serena a few nights ago to ask how things were going with her latest beau, her reply had been *really good* with a big smiley face. She'd also used other mundane words, like *great guy* and *really nice*, which sounded boring as hell. The guy sounded like a certified yawner to him.

"Looking for someone?" Aiden asked.

Dylan shifted his gaze back to his brother. "No," he lied. "Why?"

Aiden smirked knowingly. "Because you keep looking at the time on your phone, then glancing toward the gate leading to the backyard for the ceremony. If you're so concerned about Serena making it to the wedding on time, you should have brought her as *your* date. As a *friend*, of course," he amended, though Dylan didn't miss the mocking inflection in his voice.

Dylan kept his expression impassive, refusing to

play into his brother's suggestion. Everyone was aware of how Serena felt about him, and they all thought he was dense for not seeing it himself, but that's where they were wrong. His friendship with her was a hard line he refused to cross, because he was definitely *not* the whole package she was searching for, and losing her was something he would never risk.

"The only thing I'm worried about is making sure there's a cold beer on tap waiting for me after this ceremony is over," he replied, just as Eric Miller, Leo's good friend and business partner, joined them.

"Did someone say cold beer?" Eric said jovially, a big grin on his face. "Point the way."

"*After* the wedding," Aiden said, sounding like the stern older brother he was.

Eric laughed and shook his head. "Jesus, being a husband and a father has made you a total stick-in-the-mud."

"No I'm not," Aiden replied, clearly annoyed by the unflattering characterization.

"Yeah, you kind of are," Dylan agreed, trying not to laugh at the offended look on his brother's face. "I mean, who plans a night of playing pool at a pub for a guy's bachelor party? Not a stripper in sight. That's the definition of a stick-in-the-mud if you ask me."

Aiden frowned at Dylan. "It's what Leo wanted."

"That's what he *said* he wanted," Eric cut in. "But

come on, you could have livened things up with a little . . . entertainment."

"And that's the difference between men who are in committed relationships with great women and boys who still want to play around," Aiden said. "We don't feel the need to gawk at strange women stripping off their clothes when we're perfectly happy and content with what we have at home."

Eric slapped Aiden good-naturedly on the back. "Don't worry about it, old man. Dylan and I are heading to Vegas next weekend and we'll more than make up for the lack of entertainment at Leo's bachelor party while we're there."

"Las Vegas?" Aiden asked curiously, glancing at Dylan. "What for?"

"I have a meeting with the marketing manager at a small boutique hotel and casino off the strip who's interested in creating an app for their guests to enhance their gambling experience. They want to hammer out the last of the details of our contract so I can get started on the project." It was another lucrative deal to add to Stone Media's list of clients. "Since Eric and I are the only single guys left, we'll go and live it up for those of you who are now wearing a ball and chain."

Aiden glanced at the beautiful woman holding their baby, then back to Dylan with a smile. "I wouldn't trade what I have with Daisy for anything, even if it does mean wearing a so-called ball and chain. You two have no idea what you're missing out on."

Dylan grinned back at his blissfully happy brother, who not so long ago would have balked at the idea of being tied down. "Who are you, and what have you done with my brother Aiden?" he teased.

"Hey, everyone," Serena's familiar voice rang out, slightly breathless and husky, drawing Dylan's attention to the direction of the feminine sound as she and her date joined their family circle, which she'd always been a part of. "We took a wrong turn and I'm glad we figured it out because I'd be crushed if I missed the ceremony."

Dylan barely held back a smirk. Clearly, her date was the directionally challenged one and had made the wrong turn, and a small, stupid part of him took pleasure in that flaw. Especially considering the man who had his hand resting very intimately on the base of Serena's spine was tall, good-looking, and well put together with no outward imperfections to be found.

As for Serena, well, she looked stunningly beautiful in a pale pink dress that was classy yet subtly sexy in the way the off-the-shoulder design exposed her smooth, creamy skin and hinted at the soft upper swells of her breasts. She'd worn her hair in an up-swept style with a few wavy strands framing her face, and Dylan was struck with the annoying thought that later tonight her date just might be the lucky bastard who got to pull out the pins holding all that soft, glorious hair in place.

"We have about ten more minutes before we have to be seated," Dylan's mother, Grace, said amicably, her gaze lighting up with interest as she gave Serena's date a curious once-over. "Who is this handsome man you're with?"

"This is Ashton Carlyle," Serena said, then went on to introduce him to each person by name, which the guy acknowledged with a friendly handshake.

Dylan was the last one to greet him, and had to admit that he had a strong, firm grip that commanded respect. Begrudgingly, Dylan gave the other man his approval as Serena's date. For now.

"Let me have that sweet girl," Serena said, taking Isabella from Daisy and holding her on one hip as she cooed nonsensical things to the baby that made Isabella's eyes widen in glee.

The little girl loved Serena and lit up whenever she saw her. And every time Dylan watched his best friend with Isabella, he felt a weird pang in his chest he did his best to ignore because he didn't want to acknowledge what it all might mean. Having babies was what Serena longed for, it was what she deserved after her own tumultuous family life, but kids were not on Dylan's radar, which was not an issue for him since he'd have plenty of nieces and nephews to spoil.

Her date, clearly uninterested in the baby, turned toward the group of guys, his gaze landing on Dylan. "Serena tells me that you're childhood friends and you grew up next to one another."

Dylan refrained, just barely, from correcting the other man about the status of their relationship, that they'd been *best friends* all their lives, and still were, but knew that would just be petty when he seemed like a decent guy. "Yep. She's a fantastic girl, so make sure you treat her right, or you'll have to answer to me," he said, joking. Sort of.

Ashton laughed lightly. "Duly noted, though I have to point out that those sexy curves of hers say she's more of a woman than a girl, so treating her right will be no problem at all," he replied, kidding right back. Sort of.

Dylan frowned at the inappropriate innuendo in his words, then told himself to lighten up and to stop trying to find fault with the guy.

"The music for the ceremony is starting, so we should take our seats," Grace suggested, and they all headed toward the wooden chairs set up on the lawn in front of a big, white gazebo decorated in white and pink flowers, where the seating for the nuptials was open and casual.

Dylan found himself seated beside Eric in the row behind his mother and Charles, Daisy and Aiden, with Serena and her date positioned directly in front of his chair. They were seated for only a few minutes before his brother, Leo, took his place up on the gazebo in front of the minister, then faced the guests as he waited for his bride to appear. The couple had opted for a small, intimate ceremony, with just close friends and family in attendance. They'd also decided to forego the fanfare of having bridesmaids and best men, which was why he, Aiden, and Eric were sitting out in the audience, which was fine with him.

Instead of having wedding-day jitters, Leo beamed like he was the luckiest man on the planet, and as soon as Dylan got a glimpse of Peyton, stunningly beautiful in a simple but elegant white wedding gown as she walked down the aisle with her father escorting her, it became obvious how much Leo adored the woman who'd made him believe in love again after being jilted a few years before.

The ceremony itself was short and sweet, and throughout the service, Dylan didn't miss the way Serena dabbed at her eyes with a tissue, or her soft sniffles as the couple exchanged their vows, or how her date took her hand and gave it a gentle, affectionate squeeze as if to let her know he was aware of her emotions and feelings.

Ugh. Okay, fine, maybe he was a nice guy after all.

After Leo and Peyton were pronounced husband and wife, and after walking back down the aisle together while everyone clapped and cheered, the couple was whisked away for photos while all the guests migrated to the other end of the yard, where appetizers and an open bar awaited them, before a sit-down dinner was served.

Dylan ended up at a table with his family, which included Serena and her date, though thankfully Ashton guided the two of them to the seats across from Dylan and beside Aiden, because Dylan wasn't in the mood to make small talk with the other man. But that didn't stop him from eavesdropping on their conversation as his brother and Serena's date exchanged work-related stories, with Aiden as an ad executive and Ashton as a pharmaceutical rep, while Serena conversed with Grace, who was seated next to her.

During the course of the meal, it didn't escape Dylan's notice that Ashton went through two gin and tonics, when he'd already consumed two others during the appetizer round. But the guy held his liquor well because his speech never wavered and he seemed in complete control of his faculties. It was impressive . . . and worrisome because Serena had ridden to the wedding with him and he was also her ride home at the end of the night.

For the rest of the evening, Dylan sat on the side-lines and continued to surreptitiously watch the other man, who always seemed to have a drink in his hand, except for the times that he was out on the dance floor with Serena, when his hands were on *her*, instead, as he whispered things that made her laugh and smile and blush in his attempt to charm the panties off of her later.

Dylan's stomach burned with . . . acid. Yeah, that's what it had to be. A case of heartburn that had nothing to do with the certain green-eyed monster lurking inside him.

While Serena was distracted watching along with everyone else as Peyton and Leo cut their cake, her date made another quick trip to the open bar and downed his drink before joining her again, keeping her oblivious to just how much alcohol he was consuming. Then they were back out on the dance floor enjoying the lively, energetic music along with the other cou-ples, including Daisy and Aiden, while his mother and Charles watched Isabella, and even Eric, who'd persuaded a guest from the bride's side of the family to join in on the fun.

Three or four songs later, Ashton and Serena took a break. As they held hands, the other man spun her around until she was laughing breathlessly, face flushed pink, then they reached the table where Dylan had been sitting and observing from afar.

"I could use a drink," Ashton said, not a hint of a slur in his speech, or any other indication that he'd imbibed too much. "Either of you want something from the bar?"

"No, thanks," Dylan said, biting his tongue to keep from saying, *Don't you think you've had enough to drink?* "I'm good."

"I'd love a water," Serena replied, smiling at her date as she sat down at the table with Dylan.

Once Ashton was out of earshot, Serena glanced at him, her expression infused with happiness. "He's a great guy, don't you think?"

God, it killed him that she wanted his approval, but her eyes were so hopeful as they waited for his reply, and Dylan exhaled a deep breath and chose his words carefully, because Serena's safety was his priority. "He seems like a perfectly nice guy, except for the fact that he's had more to drink than anyone else here tonight."

That sparkle in her eyes dimmed a bit as she frowned at him. "He's not drunk, if that's what you're insinuating."

Again, Dylan took a moment to evaluate his thoughts before speaking. "Drunk is a relative term. Is he sloppy drunk and slurring his words and can't keep his balance? No, he's not. But he's had seven drinks tonight and is currently ordering his eighth, which to me indicates a problem."

Her gaze shifted to the bar, to the man who was already gulping down the liquor the bartender had just delivered in a glass. "Oh. I had no idea," she said quietly. "I mean, I wasn't really paying attention and he's not showing any signs of being inebriated."

At least now she was aware of the situation, even if he'd pretty much burst her bubble and put a damper on her evening. "He holds his liquor well enough that most people wouldn't know he's probably extremely intoxicated. And the fact that he can drink that much and act fine means he's an experienced drinker."

Ashton started their way, holding a glass of water in his hand, his own drink already gone, and Dylan knew he needed to say one more thing, and quickly, before the other man arrived. "I just want you to be aware of the situation so you can be careful and make a smart decision about leaving with him tonight. In fact, I think you should be the one to drive the two of you home. Or if you're not comfortable with that, then you know you can count on me to give you a ride."

She nodded, doing her best to conceal her disappointment just as her date appeared at their table and handed her the glass of water she'd requested. She took a sip, her gaze studying Ashton above the rim, and it was obvious to Dylan that she was now looking at the other man in a whole new light. And he honestly felt bad . . . yet there was no way in hell that he'd allow Serena to get into a vehicle with this guy when his blood alcohol level was undoubtedly way over legal limits.

Soon after that, the bride and groom took off for their wedding night together, and the guests gradually started to disperse. Dylan was standing with Eric, trying to convince him to be a beta tester for The Boyfriend Experience app before it officially launched—with Eric balking at the idea of being some woman's ideal date—while the rest of the family gathered up their things so they could leave, as well.

Ashton and Serena joined them, her expression troubled now that she was aware of his drinking habits, though her date didn't seem to notice her more subdued demeanor as he slid his hand into hers.

"It was great meeting all of you," Ashton said, his tone steady and polite, despite the glassy look of his eyes. "I think we're going to head out for the night."

"You two have a good evening," Grace said, smiling at them and oblivious to Serena's uneasy demeanor.

After a round of goodbyes, Dylan waited for Serena to say something to her date, but instead she started to walk away with him. The last thing Dylan wanted to do was interfere, but the thought of something happening to her as a result of Ashton's reckless behavior had him stepping forward, intending to stop them, just as Serena did the same.

He waited and watched as Serena withdrew her hand from Ashton's, and her date gave her a quizzical look.

"Is something wrong?" he asked.

She swallowed nervously. "I think I should drive you home tonight." Her voice was low in an attempt to keep things private between them, but Dylan was close enough to hear . . . and see the stiffening of Ashton's body.

"Is there a reason why?" Now his tone was defensive and just on the edge of being belligerent. As if he knew exactly where this conversation was heading and was preparing himself for a fight.

"Because I think it's the smart thing to do considering how much you've had to drink," she said quietly but kindly.

He scoffed at her. "I'm fine, and I don't appreciate you being the alcohol police and telling me how much is too much for me to drink. I'm a grown man, for crying out loud."

Serena's chin tipped up in that stubborn way of hers, and she held out her hand toward him. "Give me your keys, Ashton. Please." Her voice was calm but firm, making Dylan proud that she was standing her ground.

Ashton smacked her hand away. "I'm not giving you my goddamn keys," he said, the hostile tone to his voice drawing curious stares from departing guests. "And you're embarrassing the shit out of me right now. Let's go." He grabbed her arm and jerked her toward the backyard gate, causing her to falter in her high-heel shoes.

A red haze of barely leashed anger flashed in front of Dylan. He wasn't normally prone to violence, but he immediately bolted forward, his temper rising as he watched Serena struggle to break free from the other man's grasp. There was no way in his lifetime that he was going to allow any guy to treat any woman, and especially his best girl, with such disrespect and aggression. *Ever.*

"Oh, fuck," he heard Aiden mutter from somewhere behind him, but his brother's concern was the least of Dylan's worries.

Reaching Ashton, who'd turned into a flaming asshole, Dylan clamped a hand down on his shoulder, forcing the other man to a stop. "Let her go." It wasn't a request, but a demand.

Ashton spun around, shrugging off Dylan's hold and tightening his grip on Serena's arm, to the point that she winced in clear discomfort. "Are you kidding me right now? I'm taking my date home."

"Do I look like I'm joking, asshole? She's not interested in going anywhere with you." Dylan wrapped his fist in the other man's shirt and pushed him back, just hard enough that Ashton stumbled and finally released Serena, enabling him to regain his balance before he fell flat on his ass.

"Don't fucking touch me," Ashton said, loudly and furiously, as he suddenly came at Dylan. Although he hadn't shown signs of being intoxicated earlier, his coordination wasn't at its best now, and Ashton's arm swung out awkwardly, yet his fist managed to clip Dylan in the jaw.

Dylan heard Serena scream his name, but with the first punch thrown, all bets were off, and Dylan hurled toward Ashton to return the shot, only to be brought up short by someone grabbing the back of his suit jacket.

"I don't think Leo would be happy to hear that his brother was in a brawl at his wedding reception," Aiden said, the big-brother voice of reason. Then, he glanced at Ashton, his tone far more direct and unyielding. "As for you, I suggest you leave the premises, or I'll be more than happy to make a call to the police and have them escort you out. It's your choice."

Ashton glared at Dylan before shifting his gaze to Serena and issuing one last nasty barb. "You're not worth the trouble." Then he stalked toward the gate leading to the front of the house and his car.

"Neither are you, pencil dick," Dylan called after him, which earned him a flip of the bird and a big 'ol *fuck you* from the other man.

Aiden shook his head. "Jesus, Dylan, *how* old are you?"

Dylan smirked at his brother, despite the slight ache in his jaw. "At the moment, fifteen."

"No shit," Aiden said with a laugh, then went to rejoin his wife, who'd moved herself and a sleeping Isabella far away from rest of the group, just in case a fight broke out.

"Oh my God, Dylan, are you okay?" Serena rushed up to him, concern knitting her brows as she touched her fingers to his jaw, where he'd taken one for the team.

Her fingers were soft and cool as they caressed the spot, and he had to admit that he liked her fussing over him way too much. "I'm good," he assured her with one of his charming, dimpled grins. "Though I might need you to kiss it and make it better," he teased.

She rolled her eyes at him. "How about I take you home and put some ice on it instead."

"Okay, but I kind of like my suggestion better," he joked, then settled his arm along her shoulders and tucked her against his side, knowing exactly how the night was going to end.

With Ben & Jerry's ice cream and Hallmark movies.

Chapter Four

B Y THE TIME Serena finished watching a sappy, romantic, albeit predictable movie with Dylan a few hours later, while listening to his funny commentary on what was going to happen between the characters *before* it happened, which admittedly made her laugh, she actually felt marginally better about the less-than-ideal way her evening with Ashton had ended.

But now here she was again, back to square one on the dating scene, which she was beginning to loathe, she thought with a sigh.

"You okay?" Dylan asked, turning down the volume on the TV.

She glanced at him and smiled, grateful that he was always there for her, that he was a man who wouldn't, and didn't, hesitate to step into a potentially volatile situation and be her knight in shining armor and defend her honor—even if he'd never return her deeper feelings for him.

"Yeah, I'll be fine. I always am, though I'm seriously thinking of hiring a private investigator to vet my future dates," she said, only half joking.

He laughed. "I've been thinking and I have an idea. Maybe you just need a palate cleanser before starting the dating process again."

She raised her brows, trying to follow his idea. "Kind of like indulging in a mint sorbet in between men to remove any lingering bad taste in my mouth so I can enjoy the next guy with a brand-new perspective?"

"Yeah, exactly like that," he said with a nod.

"Okay, I'm listening."

He shifted on the chaise part of the couch where he was reclining to better face her, causing the muscles in his arms and stomach to flex. When they'd both arrived at Dylan's place, the first thing they'd done was change out of the dressy clothes they'd worn for the wedding. Like always, she'd picked one of his comfy T-shirts to slip into, and he'd returned to the living room in a pair of gray cotton shorts. The fact that his chest was bare made him temptation personified, and during the course of the movie, she'd casually looked her fill of his lean, toned abdomen and that trail of dark hair that provided an enticing path to parts of his body she'd only fantasized about. A lot.

"So, Eric and I are heading to Las Vegas next

weekend," he said, forcing her attention back to what he was saying. "Mainly, it's because I have a meeting with the marketing manager at the Sapphire Casino and Hotel to finalize the contract on the app Stone Media is creating for them and their guests. It's a quick, one-night, turnaround trip. We're arriving Saturday morning around nine so I'm there for my one o'clock meeting, and we're leaving Sunday afternoon. Why don't you and Chelsea come with?"

A frivolous weekend away from the same old grind sounded fabulous. "Are you serious?"

He gave her a cute, lopsided smile and slid his index finger down the slope of her nose in a playful manner. "I wouldn't ask if I wasn't serious, silly girl. You and Chelsea would have your own room for the night, and you can hang out at the pool or indulge in some retail therapy or do a spa day and just relax and rejuvenate while I'm taking care of business. Then, once I'm done with my appointment, it's playtime in Sin City for the four of us. I've already been comped dinner tickets at Sapphire's five-star restaurant, and we can check out the night club they just opened. Who knows, you just might find the man of your dreams there."

She laughed at that. "Doubtful." Because the man of her dreams was sitting right in front of her, oblivious to her feelings for him.

"What do you think?" he asked.

"I think it sounds great . . . as long as Chelsea and I won't be cramping your and Eric's style?" The last thing she wanted to be was a tagalong.

"Not at all," he said, and she knew him well enough to know that he was being honest. "I think it'll be fun. Just four friends hanging out, gambling, and maybe even being a little wild and crazy in a place where nobody knows us."

It had been a long time since Serena had let her hair down, so to speak. In fact, she couldn't even remember the last time she'd just let loose, without analyzing the consequences. She'd always been the quintessential good girl compared to her sister, always responsible and focused, and never coloring outside the lines because she'd had her life laid out in front of her in a particular order. Graduate from high school. Move out on her own while attending college and getting her teaching degree. Establish her career . . . and get married so she could have babies and a family of her own.

Yeah, that last part wasn't falling into place like she'd imagined, she thought with that too familiar frustration and disappointment. But for one weekend, before she continued her quest for Mr. Right, she just wanted to be a little carefree, spontaneous, and uninhibited and not be so straight-laced, and what better place to do that than Vegas?

"Okay, we'll go," she said, excited at all the possibilities that awaited her. And if she was lucky, Vegas was going to be the place she got her groove back.

RETAIL THERAPY HAD never been Serena's thing, mostly because she couldn't bring herself to spend money impulsively. She was too sensible and practical, and there were always those painful memories that lingered from childhood, of her mother buying things she couldn't afford, but always worrying about paying for rent, the utilities, and food. There had been times when the latter had been sparse, and Serena had been fortunate that Dylan's mom would insist on her eating dinner with the family, but it taught her to be smart with her finances, and that meant purchasing things at a discount, or when they were on sale. She rarely paid full price for anything.

Chelsea, however, didn't have that same separation anxiety with money as she did, and every time her friend whipped out her credit card for a purchase in one of the upscale designer boutiques located in the forum shops in Caesars Palace in Las Vegas, Serena cringed and went into sticker shock at the total amount displayed on the register.

They'd only been in Vegas for a few hours, but as

soon as their plane had touched down, Chelsea had dragged her off to shop for a few hours, while Dylan and Eric had gone to the Sapphire Casino and Hotel to check in, and for Dylan's meeting with the marketing manager. They'd promised to all meet up at five for dinner, then on to the nightclub for an evening of cocktails and dancing. Which left Serena and Chelsea a good six hours to fill.

"Aren't you going to try on anything at all?" Chelsea asked, her hands already ladened with shopping bags.

"You're kidding me, right?" Serena asked, raising a brow at her friend as they strolled past Tiffany's, then the storefront for Dior. "Do you not know me at all?"

"Yes, I know your spending habits, or lack thereof," she teased, bumping her shoulder against Serena's. "But here's a concept for you. Live a little, and for the weekend, stop taking everything so seriously. Just because you try on an outfit doesn't mean *you* have to buy it. But we're in Vegas, and when will you ever get the chance to wear a hot, slinky, one-of-a-kind gorgeous dress like that? Just for fun?"

Serena followed the direction of Chelsea's pointing finger to a mannequin in a window display that was wearing a stunning body-hugging dress that was definitely nightclub appropriate. "It's gorgeous," she murmured.

Chelsea grabbed her wrist and pulled her into the store before Serena could protest. "Come on, you're trying it on. Just for fun, and because Vegas is all about having fun and being daring, right?"

"Right," a young, modelesque saleswoman replied with a grin before Serena could utter a word. "You only live once, so embrace the spontaneity."

Serena refrained from rolling her eyes, knowing that the girl was angling for a sale and doing her best to convince her and Chelsea to indulge. Which wasn't going to happen.

"Exactly!" Chelsea said, as if she and the other woman shared a brain and thought the same way. "My friend would like to try on that sparkly beige dress in the window."

Serena shook her head. "I really shouldn't."

"Oh, you definitely *should*," the saleslady refuted as she walked over to a rack holding various sizes of the same outfit. "Because that dress was made for a body like yours."

Before Serena could put up an argument, she was being ushered into a large changing room, along with the dress and a matching pair of designer shoes because Chelsea wanted to see how everything looked together—for fun, she insisted once again.

Serena sort of felt bad that she was taking up the saleswoman's time when it wasn't going to result in a sale. But as she put on the luxurious but overpriced dress, which slid over her body like it had been made specifically for her curves, and secured her feet into the surprisingly comfortable black strappy heels, then looked at her reflection in the mirror, she had to admit that she was stunned by how hot and sexy she looked.

From breasts to thighs, the material molded to her body in a way no other dress in her closet ever had. The bodice was cut into a deep vee in front that showed off her cleavage, and the top was held up by spaghetti straps that crisscrossed along her bare back so that she couldn't wear a bra. With every move she made, the tiny champagne-colored sequins shimmered seductively, and the heels accentuated her long, toned legs. She felt like a million bucks, which was probably the equivalent of the shoes and dress put together.

"Hurry up, already," Chelsea called out impatiently from the waiting room. "I want to see!"

"I'm coming, I'm coming!"

Serena walked out of the changing room into the sitting area, and Chelsea gasped when she saw her.

"Wow." Her friend's eyes widened with shock. "You look . . . just . . . wow."

A laughed escaped Serena. "I don't think I've ever seen you so speechless before."

"I don't think I've ever seen you in something so provocative before," Chelsea bantered back as her gaze took in the entire outfit. "Now *that* is a Vegas dress, as well as an I'm-looking-to-get-laid dress."

"Oh, definitely," the saleslady agreed with an eager-to-make-a-sale nod. "You look so hot."

The last thing Serena was searching for on this trip was to have a one-night stand with a stranger, which wasn't her style, anyway. And it didn't matter what the dress and shoes conveyed, because she'd only tried them on *for fun*. But as she looked at herself one more time in the full-length mirror in the waiting area, she couldn't help but wish she could wear the outfit tonight, because she was curious if it would illicit any kind of reaction from Dylan.

Probably not, she thought with a disappointed sigh, because when Dylan looked at her, he only saw one thing. His best friend. And not the woman who was hopelessly, stupidly in love with him.

She returned to the changing room and removed the dress and shoes, and when the saleslady knocked on her door and requested the items, Serena slipped them through the crack in the door, figuring the other woman wanted to get them back out on display. She finished putting on her plain, practical T-shirt, jeans, and a pair of sandals and met Chelsea out front.

"Ready to go?" her friend asked.

"Yep." Serena turned to the woman who'd been so patient with them and gave her a small wave. "Thank you for your time."

"Sure thing," the saleswoman said cheerfully. "Enjoy your dress and shoes."

Wait . . . what? Just outside the store, Serena came to an abrupt halt as the other woman's words sank in. Then she glanced down and saw a new bag added to the others that Chelsea had been holding prior to them entering the shop.

Her jaw nearly dropped to the ground. "Oh my God, tell me you did *not* just buy that outfit!"

Chelsea blinked at her much too innocently. "Of course I didn't . . . Dylan did."

"Dylan?" Serena glanced around, expecting to see her best guy friend lurking nearby, but he was nowhere to be found. In fact, this was about the time he was supposed to be getting ready for his important business meeting. "He's not even here. How is that possible?"

Now, Chelsea looked a little impish. "He gave me his credit card after we landed at the airport, when you were in the restroom, and told me to make sure you bought yourself something fun and Vegas appropriate to wear tonight. I think we accomplished that task, don't you?"

"I don't think Dylan was anticipating spending what those two items cost." She ran her fingers through her hair, her stomach cramping at how much

Chelsea had just spent. "It's ridiculous and I need to take them back."

"You will do no such thing." Chelsea walked to a nearby bench and sat on one side while unburdening her hands of all the shopping bags she was hauling around. "Sit down."

Serena frowned at her friend but settled in for their disagreement. Before she could say anything, Chelsea spoke.

"Look, Dylan said you'd be stubborn about it, so no big shock there. And I figured making the purchase on the sly was the easiest way to achieve the goal without having an argument between us in the store in front of people. He wanted to do this for you, and he said if it made you feel any better, you could consider it your birthday present."

Serena arched a dubious brow. "My birthday isn't for another four months."

"Eh, it's all a matter of semantics," Chelsea refuted with a shrug. "It's a gift that Dylan wanted to give to you, so just embrace it instead of being so resistant."

Serena exhaled a deep breath and forced her stiff shoulders to relax. On one hand, she was touched that Dylan wanted to do something so sweet, but there was that part of her that thought about his ex-girlfriend, Brandy, and how she'd taken advantage of what was in Dylan's bank account to offset the fact that he hadn't given her the emotional attention she'd craved. Serena wasn't that kind of girl, and never would be, but it was also difficult for her to accept such a luxurious, expensive gift for no reason at all—because she certainly didn't believe his excuse about buying it for her birthday.

Chelsea put her hand on Serena's arm, bringing her back to their conversation. "I say you wear the outfit and enjoy the sexy, confident way it makes you feel. You deserve that after . . . well, the whole debacle with Ashton," she said with a cringe, since she'd been partially responsible for introducing her to the guy. "Let's meet Dylan and Eric for dinner, then go to the nightclub and live it up for the evening, because I can guarantee that one look and guys are going to flock to you. And even better, you can show Dylan what he's missing out on."

Serena laughed derisively at that, because Chelsea knew all about her unrequited love for Dylan. "You can't miss what you've never wanted," she said of his platonic feelings for her.

A knowing smile curved Chelsea's lips. "Trust me. He's a guy with a dick. And best friend zone or not, he's going to notice your perky boobs and firm ass in that dress. He'd have to be dead or impotent not to, and I really don't think he's either," she teased.

"Whatever." Serena waved a hand between them,

dismissing that possibility when she'd never seen Dylan look at her with anything more than affection. She just didn't inspire desire, lust, or passion when it came to him . . . except in her own fantasies.

"Okay, you win," she said, because she clearly wasn't going to get the upper hand in this difference of opinion. "I'll wear the outfit and solemnly swear that I'll have a good time while doing it."

Chelsea beamed triumphantly. "I knew you'd see things my way. Now let's head back to the hotel and enjoy a few spa treatments before we meet the boys for dinner."

Chapter Fi e

"**D**AMN, I COULD get used to this VIP treatment."

Dylan had to agree with Eric as he leaned back in his leather chair and glanced out the floor-to-ceiling window next to him that offered a spectacular view of the Las Vegas strip. The two of them had just been seated in a private area of the five-star restaurant located on the fortieth floor of the Sapphire Casino and Hotel, where an expensive bottle of champagne was already chilling in a silver ice bucket—to celebrate the contract he'd just signed with the company, the hostess informed him before leaving them with their menus.

His meeting with the marketing manager had gone exceptionally well, and Dylan was excited to get back to San Diego, work out the last of the glitches on the Boyfriend Experience app that was frustrating the hell out of him, while starting on the framework for the Sapphire Casino and Hotel app, which was most likely going to take a few months to complete since it was such a large and intricate job.

As they waited for Serena and Chelsea to arrive, Dylan returned his gaze to Eric, trying once again to persuade him to be a guinea pig for his current project. "So, what's it going to take to convince you to be one of the beta testers for the Boyfriend Experience? I really need someone I trust giving me reliable feedback on the app before it's released to the public, and since you're single and available, you're the perfect guy for the job."

"How about a million dollars?" Eric said, his tone completely serious before his face broke out with a grin. "Oh, wait, I don't need the money, or anything else for that matter. I'm telling you, there is no bribe large enough that would entice me to sign on to a dating app when I do just fine on my own."

"It's not a normal social app like Bumble or Tinder," he corrected Eric, and not for the first time. "It's not about hooking up and getting laid, but rather standing in as boyfriend material for a woman who needs a short-term date."

"No sex?" Eric shook his head, as if the concept was foreign to him. "Then what's the point? Why would I want to risk ending up with some fatal attraction kind of date, with no guaranteed payout?"

"Okay, fine," Dylan said, realizing that Eric wasn't

going to give in or agree. "But trust me, this app is going to be huge once it launches."

"Yeah, okay . . ." Eric's voice trailed off as his gaze seemed to focus on something over Dylan's shoulder. "Jesus Christ. I think we're looking at double trouble coming right at us."

Dylan turned his head to see what Eric was talking about and felt his mouth go dry at the sight of Serena and Chelsea being led their way by the hostess. But it was Serena who held his full, riveted attention, because holy shit, she looked like a certified goddess in a pale gold, shimmering dress that outlined her centerfold curves. Lush breasts. Nipped-in waist and the flare of her hips. And long, slender legs that ended in a pair of four-inch heels with straps that wrapped provocatively around her ankles.

She'd worn her hair down in soft waves that fell over her bare shoulders, with the ends teasing the upper swells of her firm breasts. Her makeup was more dramatic and smoky hued than her normally fresh-faced look, her chest and arms dusted with the tiniest flecks of gold, and there was a sultry confidence to her walk that made his dick sit up and take notice.

Eric jabbed him in the side with his elbow, knocking Dylan out of his stupor. "You might want to pick up your jaw off the floor before the girls get to the table. It's not polite to drool in public."

Dylan snapped his mouth shut, but the heated buzz of awareness sluicing through his veins wasn't so easily diverted. It just kept heading inappropriately south until the front of his pants felt way too tight. Jesus, keeping his attraction to Serena concealed on a regular basis was difficult enough, but this bombshell had his hormones flipping into overdrive.

"Look out, gentlemen," Chelsea said with flair as the two of them arrived. "I convinced Serena to embrace her wild side tonight."

The girls sat down, with Chelsea taking the chair next to Eric and Serena settling into the one next to him as the hostess placed menus in front of them, then left them alone. The scent of whatever perfume Serena was wearing seduced his senses further, and it was all he could do to keep his eyes on her beautiful face, instead of the creamy swells of her breasts.

He tried hard not to acknowledge the fact that this version of his best friend had him more than a little hot and bothered. "Serena doesn't have a wild side that I know of." Okay, yeah, maybe that wasn't the best thing to say, because he didn't care for the daring arch of her brow as she met his gaze.

"Are you insinuating that I'm boring?"

Yep. There was a definite challenge in that question. "Not boring, per se. Just . . . conservative. That dress is indecent compared to anything I've ever seen you wear." So much so that he had to resist the urge to take off his jacket and cover her up with it so no other guy had the chance to ogle her. He was sure this was his punishment for giving Chelsea free rein with his credit card to buy an outfit for Serena.

Amusement shifted across her face. "Indecent? Really?"

"Do *not* answer that, bro," Eric cut in quickly, laughter in his voice. "Trust me, it's a trap. There is no right answer, and you're going to dig yourself in deeper than you already are."

Dylan chose to ignore Eric. "You look . . . beautiful," he said instead, hoping that would diffuse the situation, but instead Serena just rolled her eyes as if he'd insulted her.

Eric groaned. "From indecent to beautiful?" he echoed incredulously. "Jesus Christ, Dylan. You're giving Serena whiplash and those are *not* the compliments these ladies are waiting for." He glanced from Serena to Chelsea, a charming smile curving his lips. "Let me set the two of you straight since this idiot doesn't know how to flatter a woman. You both look fucking *hot* and *sexy*."

Both girls beamed as though Eric had bestowed riches upon them. "Thank you," they said at the same time.

Much to Dylan's relief, their waiter arrived, shifting

the conversation to the evening's specials while he opened the champagne and filled everyone's glasses with the bubbly wine. Once everyone placed their orders and the other man was gone, Serena glanced at him and picked up her flute.

"So, do we have something to celebrate tonight?" she asked curiously, her peach-hued lips glossy and enticing in the dim lighting. "Like a signed contract?"

"Yes, we do." They all lifted their glasses and toasted to his success, and after he gave the girls the key details of the meeting, Chelsea started chatting with Eric . . . or rather continued flirting with him, which had started at the airport this morning.

Serena turned her attention to him, her eyes soft and appreciative. "Thank you for buying me the dress and shoes today, even if you weren't there at the store to approve of the purchase."

There was a wry note to her voice, and he knew she was referring back to his stupid *indecent* remark, which he suddenly wanted to make up for. "I really do approve. The dress looks amazing on you."

Her bright, happy smile was like pure sunshine. "Thank you." She self-consciously touched her fingers to her chest and drew them down to where her cleavage started. "You know, this dress isn't normally me, or anything close to what I'd buy for myself."

"I know." Which was why the whole package was

so fucking sexy and had him feeling possessive and protective and all out of sorts. "But I'm glad you spoiled yourself." Which was something she rarely ever did.

"Well, you really shouldn't have," she said, her tone sincere.

"Why not?" he asked, watching her take a drink of her champagne, then lick a droplet from her bottom lip that made him thirsty as hell for the same taste.

"Because it was a *lot* of money."

"I know," he said with a laugh. "I got the credit card alert text on my phone when the charge went through."

She winced, as if the thought of the cost physically hurt her. "I'm so sorry."

"I swear I didn't say that to make you feel bad." God, what the fuck was wrong with him and his choice of words tonight? Trying to make up for being an ass, he reached out and placed his hand over hers on the table, noticing the way her lips parted and her eyes went soft at his touch. "You're worth it, Serena." He meant it. Besides, the outfit had barely put a dent in his bank account.

A light frown furrowed her brows. "I don't ever want you to feel that I'm taking advantage of you, or your money . . . like Brandy did."

He understood her concern because that whole

situation had put a sour taste in his mouth when it came to dating women, but Serena was the last person who'd ever use him for his financial status, let alone want tangible things from him because he now had more money that he knew what to do with.

"The difference is, I *want* to spoil you," he said, speaking the truth, "while Brandy expected me to spend money on her because I had it."

And admittedly, he'd indulged her because, quite frankly, Dylan now realized that he hadn't been there for her emotionally, and it had been his way of making up for his lack of attention. But she'd taken advantage, until Serena had pointed out what, exactly, was happening and forced him to make the easy decision to end the relationship. Since then, he'd had a few other dates who'd expected him to dole out money on expensive items, which was now a huge red flag for him, and it was just easier to keep things casual from the beginning.

Their waiter arrived with their dinner orders, and as they ate the fantastic gourmet meals made by a Michelin star chef, Dylan and Serena joined in on the debate that Chelsea and Eric were in the middle of having over the latest episode of *Survivor* and the contestant who had been eliminated.

Over an hour later, with their stomachs full and the bottle of champagne consumed, they headed out of the restaurant, with Chelsea and Serena walking ahead of him and Eric, who was blatantly staring at Chelsea's ass, while Dylan tried not to do the same with Serena. He'd already looked at her breasts so many times tonight that he knew he was going to hell for all the impure thoughts he'd had of her in that dress, and out of it, during dinner.

"It's too early to go to the nightclub," Chelsea said, checking the time on her phone. "Things don't really get started until after ten, so how about we head down to the casino and do some gambling for a while?"

They all agreed, and a few minutes later, Chelsea and Eric were veering off toward the poker tables, while Serena followed him to the roulette table, which was his preferred method of gambling. With only a few people currently playing, Dylan easily found a spot at the table.

"I'll watch and cheer you on," Serena said, standing a bit off to the side and out of the way.

"No, you're going to play, too," he insisted, and as she opened her mouth to say that she didn't want to risk losing her money, he gave her a pointed look. "I'm going to spot you a hundred, and don't argue with me. You're here this weekend to have fun, and you can't go to Vegas and not gamble."

She bit her bottom lip uncertainly, though he could see she really wanted to play, too. "What if I lose all of it?"

He refrained from rolling his eyes, because he knew her worry was real, and came up with the best compromise he could at the spur of the moment. "Then you owe me a week of home-cooked meals." It was a fair trade considering his cooking skills were crap.

She thought about his suggestion for a moment. "Okay, deal," she said, and he was pretty sure that the champagne from dinner was partially responsible for making her more agreeable.

Excited now, she came up beside him while he pulled two one-hundred-dollar bills from his wallet and put them on the table for the attendant to exchange into casino chips. While the croupier started the roulette wheel and spun the silver ball, the few people at the table started placing their bets. Dylan was methodical in his approach, while Serena didn't seem to have any rhyme or reason as to where she put her chips. But in the long run, it didn't seem to matter because she was lady luck, while he was shit out of luck. As her pile of chips grew, his quickly depleted until he had to toss another hundred on the table.

Because of Serena's excitement and cheering, she drew other gamblers to the table, one of whom was a guy who parked himself on the other side of her to play. Then the two of them started chatting and laughing, and Dylan clenched his jaw, hating the way Serena smiled at him and the interested way the guy looked at her. When Dylan caught the other man's gaze drifting down to her cleavage, he had to forcibly tamp down the irritation—okay, fine, *jealousy*—that was bubbling up inside him.

A few plays later, while the roulette wheel was spinning, Serena reached out to put her chips on the double zeros but couldn't quite reach. Before Dylan could help, the too friendly guy took her bet and placed it for her. Go figure, she was the only person who won that round based on her random wager. As Serena clapped enthusiastically, the stranger not-so-innocently placed his hand on her bare back, then slid his palm down to the base of her spine, and Dylan blew a fucking gasket.

"Mind getting your hand off of her ass," he snapped, meeting the other man's startled gaze with what he knew was a pissed-off glare. "She's with me tonight." Oh, shit, he hadn't meant for that last part to slip out.

Serena's gaze swiveled around to his, wide with shock.

The guy immediately lifted both of his hands in the air, his expression legitimately contrite. "Sorry, man. I didn't know." He picked up his remaining chips and went to a nearby craps table.

"Ready to cash out?" Dylan said gruffly, before she could call him out on what a jackass he'd just been, which was beginning to become the norm for him tonight, all because of the goddamn attention-grabbing dress and fuck-me heels that had men salivating over her.

Much to his relief, she let it go and picked up her winnings. "Yeah, sure."

They walked to the cashier cage and exchanged their chips into dollar bills. Serena collected her proceeds and turned to him with a huge smile.

"Oh my God, I almost doubled the money you gave me!"

She returned the hundred he'd lent her, and even though he didn't want it back, Dylan didn't argue because he knew it would be pointless. He was actually bummed that she'd won, because he'd been really looking forward to a week of home-cooked meals.

They started toward the poker tables, where Chelsea and Eric were still playing, and Serena glanced at him with a sly smile.

"So, I'm with *you* for the night, hmm?" she teased, bringing up his possessive, out-of-character behavior back at the roulette table.

He smirked and tried to make light of the situation. "Yep. Bought and paid for . . . Well, the outfit, anyway." When both of her brows raised at his sexist comment, he groaned at the fact that he'd just put *both* feet in his mouth this time. Not only that, but he was certain he was giving her mixed signals about his attraction to her.

She stopped in between two rows of slot machines and faced him, her gaze narrowed slightly. "So, are you saying the outfit comes with a price, which is my attention for the night?"

He flashed a charming, dimpled grin because this conversation was not going in a positive direction and he was desperate to smooth things over and get things back on track. "Since when is spending the evening with your best friend a hardship?"

"It's never been a hardship, Dylan," she said, the tone of her voice taking on a bit of frustration. "But tonight, I don't want this gorgeous, sexy dress and the way I feel in it to go to waste on someone who isn't going to thoroughly enjoy it."

Which meant she intended to find a guy who *would* appreciate the outfit. With that declaration ringing in his ears, she turned around and sashayed toward the poker tables, drawing the heated, interested stares of the opposite sex as she walked by. The wolves smiled at her, and she returned the sentiment, making it clear she was single and available.

Fuck him. It was going to be a long night.

Chapter Six

"WHAT'S UP WITH Dylan?" Chelsea asked as they used the mirror in the ladies' lounge to check their hair and makeup before heading back out into the nightclub fray. "He's been acting moody since the two of you met Eric and me at the poker table. Now, he's sitting by the bar scowling over . . . well, I have no idea what he's brooding about."

Serena laughed. After two very strong cocktails, she was feeling really good, and refused to let Dylan's weird attitude put a damper on her evening. "I think he's scowling because of me. Or rather, something that happened that involved me at the roulette table."

"Oh, do tell," Chelsea said, her tone intrigued as she opened her compact and powdered her face.

While touching up her lip gloss, Serena told her what had happened, along with Dylan's domineering reaction to another guy touching her. "I don't get it. He's got this whole Jekyll-and-Hyde thing going on tonight. And right now, he's all Mr. Hyde."

Chelsea smiled knowingly. "It's the dress. It's clearly bringing out the conflicted beast in him. Dylan wants you, but he's fighting the desire because of the whole BFF thing he's pigeonholed you into. And he's hating that other guys are lusting after you when he can't have you."

It was hard for Serena to wrap her mind around that concept when Dylan had never openly shown that kind of interest in her. "He's never seen me as anything more than a best friend."

"Care to test that theory?" Chelsea dared.

A part of her was tempted to do just that. "How?"

Chelsea dropped her compact back into her little purse, her eyes sparkling devilishly. "Find a guy and go out on that dance floor and dance like you're a stripper... minus the taking-off-your-clothes part, of course," she said with a laugh. "If that doesn't unhinge Dylan and get a reaction out of him, then he's never going to take you out of the friend zone. In the meantime, I'm going to go dance with Eric like *I'm* a stripper, and if I'm lucky, the clothes *will* be coming off tonight."

She waggled her brows, and Serena was pretty sure that Chelsea and Eric would be hooking up at some point tonight. There was a definite attraction between them, and neither one was looking for anything serious, so why not?

They headed out of the ladies' room, the obnoxiously loud techno music making Serena's whole body vibrate with the beat. She considered Chelsea's advice to head right out onto the dance floor with some random guy, but she wanted to give Dylan one more opportunity to stop being a grouch and have some fun, because everyone was having a great time but him when he should be celebrating the contract he'd signed earlier.

She found him sitting alone at the small round table where he'd been since they'd arrived, and he watched her approach, his eyes hooded and his expression less than inviting. But one of his cantankerous dispositions had never scared her off before, and she wasn't going to be deterred now.

Reaching the table and standing across from Dylan, she placed her hands on the wood surface and bent toward him so he could hear her over the loud music. His gaze dropped briefly to the breasts that were now eye level for him, before his jaw visibly tightened and he lifted his gaze to hers.

"Dance with me?" she asked in a playful, cajoling tone that did nothing to soften his features.

He swirled the amber liquid in his glass and shook his head. "No, thanks," he said, his voice rough around the edges. "Not in the mood."

It was the third time she'd asked him tonight, and

it was now the last. "Okay, Mr. Grumpy Pants," she said, straightening again. "I *am* in the mood, so I guess I'll have to go and find someone else who is, too."

She reached for his drink and finished whatever was inside in two gulps, ignoring the burn of liquor down her throat because she was going to need the liquid fortitude for what she was going to do next—dance like she was a stripper.

IT DIDN'T TAKE Serena long to find a willing partner, and as Dylan watched her and some guy out on the dance floor, his stomach twisted into a knot of conflicting emotions, with envy and lust topping the list He was also feeling possessive—like, caveman-level possessive—which he had no right to be. Serena was free to do whatever she wanted with the stranger, even if Dylan wanted her for himself.

And right now, she was dancing like she had zero inhibitions left, which was the first time he'd ever seen her so brazen and openly sensual when she was usually much more modest and reserved. Her body was loose and fluid, despite the four-inch heels she was wearing. Her hips swayed provocatively in that sexy, shimmering dress, and the sultry, inviting smile she bestowed on the muscle head she was with made Dylan clench his jaw, hard.

It was complete torture to witness her seducing some random guy, to think about the possibility that she might do something completely out of character for her after having a few cocktails—like leave with her dance partner and have a one-night stand. And considering how cozy the two of them seemed to be getting, that scenario worried him more with each passing minute.

The song segued into another, and the guy she was with grew bolder, more daring with his touches. He looped an arm around her waist and anchored Serena up against his body, and much to Dylan's dismay, she looped her hands around his neck and followed his lead in a dirty dance that set him on edge. When the man's hands drifted down to grab her ass so he could grind against her, Dylan shot out of his chair and reached the couple in record speed, and just like earlier at the roulette table, he asserted himself—to protect her from doing something potentially stupid with a total stranger. Never mind his own personal envy issues.

He gently but firmly grabbed Serena's arm and pried the two apart. She looked up at him with wide, startled eyes, and the guy shot him a dark, irritated glance meant to dissuade Dylan from poaching on what he believed was now his territory.

"What the hell, man?" the muscle head said

gruffly. "You need to back off and find your own woman to dance with. This one's mine."

The fact that the guy referred to Serena as a possession rankled Dylan even more. "Actually, she's *mine*," he said, staking his own claim. "She's here with me."

The other man's gaze shifted to Serena. "Are you? Here with him?"

She sighed in resignation, and even though Dylan knew she wasn't happy with his interference once again, she made her choice, and thank God it was *him*. "Yes, I am."

Relief flooded through him. She could have said no. She could have outed him as a friend. She could have blown him off and walked out of the nightclub with the guy, but Dylan knew that wasn't Serena's style or MO. That this flashy, wanton Vegas persona wasn't her in real life, and had most likely been an act to make him sweat. Well, the joke was on her because if that had been her ploy, she definitely had his attention.

"You could have told me earlier," the guy muttered, then stalked off the dance floor, leaving Dylan and Serena facing one another.

She braced her hands on her hips, her eyes now flashing with annoyance. "That's the second time tonight you scared off a guy. You can't keep doing that."

"Yes, I can," he argued. "I invited you to Vegas, so you *are* with me."

Understanding dawned across her expression. "Are you trying to cock block me?" she asked incredulously.

One hundred percent yes. "No. You've asked me to dance. Three times. I'm here. Now let's dance."

He barked the words out like an order, and instead of irritating Serena, a devious smile curved her lips, and she did exactly what he'd asked, but in a way they'd never danced before. In previous situations, dancing together had been all platonic, wholesome, friendly fun with teasing and laughing and busting out some of the latest dance moves to keep things light and entertaining.

Not so tonight. Tonight, she was embracing her inner bad girl, when she'd always been the quintessential good girl, which made the transformation even more arousing. There was nothing innocent or chaste about the way Serena moved her body to the beat of the music, or how she lifted the hair from the back of her neck and executed a slow, sensual shimmy that made his dick excruciatingly hard. She closed her eyes, tipped her head back, and caressed her hands along the sides of her breasts and down her hips, then turned around and brushed her curvy bottom against the front of his pants, causing a dozen dirty, filthy thoughts to trample through his brain.

Fucking hell. She was deliberately taunting him, testing to see just how far she could push his limits before his restraint totally snapped. She was close to achieving her goal. So fucking close it took every ounce of effort he possessed to keep his hands to himself, instead of securing his arm around her waist, anchoring her body tight to his, and grinding his aching cock against her ass and shocking the hell out of her with his blatant erection when she believed he was immune to her as a desirable, fuckable woman.

After three agonizingly long songs, Dylan was desperate to put distance between them. "I think it's time we call it a night," he said, glancing around the club for Eric and Chelsea but not finding either one.

"I thought you wanted to dance," she said, and he didn't miss the sassy, mocking tone to her voice as she raised her hands above her head and swiveled her hips way too sensually.

Oh, yeah, she was totally yanking his chain. "We danced, it's almost midnight, and now it's time to go."

"I don't turn into a pumpkin at midnight, so I'm good." She gave him a little finger wave as she continued to dance. "You go right ahead, though, and I'll see you in the morning when it's time to leave for the airport."

He shook his head adamantly. "I'm not leaving you here by yourself."

She blinked at him guilelessly. "Why not? I'm a big girl, Dylan."

"Because you've had a few drinks," he said, stating the obvious.

"You don't trust my judgment?"

She finally stopped moving, her face beautifully flushed, just how he'd always imagined she'd look after sex. *Stop fucking thinking about sex with her, asshole, because your dick can't take much more visual stimulation.*

"No, I don't trust the men here not to take advantage of you," he replied honestly. "I can't find Chelsea and Eric, so I'd feel much better knowing you were safe and sound in your room for the night and not in this nightclub alone."

"Fine, Mr. Grumpy Pants," she said for the second time this evening, which only made him grumpier. "It was fun while it lasted."

Grateful she'd agreed, he took her hand and they made their way through the crowded club. Once outside the venue, he released his hold on her and they walked quietly to the bank of elevators, where a whole group of people shuffled into the lift behind them, squishing Dylan and Serena into the back corner.

Her warmth and scent wreaked havoc on his senses with every breath he took. He was still on edge from her rubbing up against him on the dance floor, and it didn't help matters that her backside was inches away from finding out just how hot and bothered she'd managed to make him. He was so excruciatingly hard his dick throbbed for relief, which sadly it wasn't going to get tonight, and he shifted his stance so his erection didn't end up prodding Serena's ass.

It seemed to take forever until they reached their floor, and they quietly walked down the hall toward their separate junior suites, which were located directly across from each other, with him and Eric on one side, and her and Chelsea on the other.

She retrieved her key card from the small purse she'd worn with the strap across her body so she didn't have to hold the bag. He started to tell her good night as she waved the plastic card in front of the lock mechanism, but the faint sounds he heard coming from inside her room—unmistakable moaning, groaning, sex noises—had him blurting out, "Don't open the door!" right as she pushed inside.

She sucked in a startled breath and froze as she belatedly realized what she'd just walked in on—their friends getting laid. With each other. Half-dressed, Eric was sitting on the couch in the living room area, with Chelsea straddling his lap, her dress hiked up to the tops of her thighs as they kissed and groped and moaned in pleasure, oblivious to the fact that they had an audience. Jesus, out of courtesy, the least they could have done was hang the do-not-disturb sign on the door.

"Oh, crap," Dylan heard Serena rasp. Clearly flustered, she spun around, and in her haste to get out of the room, she slammed right into him as the door shut behind her.

The unexpected impact had her wobbling on her heels, and his hands automatically shot out to grab her arms, then hauled her close to keep her steady on her feet.

Big fucking mistake. Not only because her sweet, firm breasts were crushed against his chest and her body plastered to his, but the big, round eyes staring up at him in shock had nothing to do with what they'd just witnessed and everything to do with the stiff length of his erection tenting his pants that was now pressing insistently against her belly.

"Oh my God, are you turned on because you just saw . . ."

Her words trailed off, but he knew what, or whom, she was referring to. The easy answer was to say yes, even if it did make him look like a pervert, but the frustration he'd been dealing with all night was at its tipping point and overrode common sense.

"No, it's because of *you*, Serena," he said through gritted teeth, the filter on his words having gone AWOL. "I've been hard as a rock since you wiggled your ass against my dick out on the dance floor. I'm a man, you're gorgeous and hot as hell, so yeah, I fucking want you."

Time stood still as the truth spilled out of him, his heart racing in his chest at what he'd just revealed. Serena's lips parted, her features etched at first with disbelief, then quickly shifting to hope and elation, then on to something more daring and courageous.

"It's now or never," he heard her whisper right before she wrapped her arms around his neck, pulled his head down to hers, and kissed him . . . not like a friend, but a sinfully sexy lover.

This couldn't happen. *Stop her*, his brain shouted as their mouths merged and her tongue touched his bottom lip enticingly . . . but the accumulation of desire he'd harbored for his best friend for so many years finally crashed through every bit of self-discipline he had left, which wasn't much at this point.

He was helpless to resist her, and he suddenly no longer wanted to.

Chapter Se en

SERENA KNEW TAKING a chance and kissing Dylan was a huge leap of faith with the outcome being a potential rejection, but after listening to him confess the reason for being so aroused—*because of her*—she'd decided to throw caution to the wind and finally just go for it. And ohmigod, once Dylan had gotten past the initial shock of the hot, intimate kiss she'd planted on him, the risk she'd taken was so worth the reward.

At the teasing touch of her tongue along his bottom lip, he groaned and framed her face in his hands and took control. Tipping her head to the side, he slanted his mouth over hers in a hot, deep, lust-driven kiss that had her entire body responding to his greedy, possessive conquest. Her nipples tightened into hard points, heat curled in her belly, and slick need dampened her panties.

Clenching her fingers in his hair, she arched against him, wanting more, *needing* more. She couldn't remember ever feeling so electrified so quickly with any other man, couldn't recall a time when she wanted to just tear a guy's clothes off because she was so impatient to feel him inside her. And judging by the thick length of Dylan's cock searing her though their clothes, there was *a lot* to feel.

She moaned softly and moved restlessly against him, rubbing her aching breasts against his chest and rolling her hips slowly and seductively, causing a deep, impatient growl to rumble in his chest. With his mouth still fused to hers, he pulled her forward while he walked backward, and she was more than willing to follow wherever he led if it meant tasting more of his dirty, sexy kisses. She felt him fumble for something in his pocket and, a moment later, heard the soft click of his hotel room door unlocking. He shoved it open with his backside, let it slam after they were both inside, then promptly pushed her up against the nearest wall.

He wedged one thigh between hers, pressing high and pinning her lower body in place as he pulled his mouth from hers and stared down at her, his eyes blazing with a blistering heat she'd never seen him direct at her before. Both of them were breathing hard, and bracing one arm above her head, he splayed his other hand at the base of her throat and caressed his thumb along the rapid beat of her pulse fluttering there.

She swallowed hard, knowing this was a defining moment between them, especially when she saw the agonizing doubts and second thoughts chasing across his expression. He closed his eyes and lightly touched his forehead to hers, his warm breath feathering across her cheek.

"Serena . . ."

His voice was ragged and torn, and wavered with uncertainties. Serena reached up and touched her fingertips to his clenched jaw, her only thought to waylay any hesitations holding him back, because she had absolutely none about him and where this was heading. It felt as though she'd waited a lifetime for this opportunity, for him to finally see her as more than just his best girl friend, and after that hungry, demanding kiss that said more about his attraction to her than words ever could, she wasn't going to let this perfect moment slip through her fingers.

"I want this," she whispered, brushing her lips against his to reinforce her statement while slipping her hands into his suit jacket and pushing it off his shoulders because she was dying to touch his bare skin in a very intimate and sexual way. "I want *you*, so please don't tell me no."

With a helpless-sounding groan, he dipped his head again and crushed his lips to hers, supplying his answer with another steamy, toe-curling, tongue-tangling, panty-melting kiss that enflamed every part of her. Sheer desperation had her shoving his jacket down his arms and off, then she yanked his shirt from his pants and eagerly unfastened the buttons all the way down his torso until she had access to his chest, his stomach. His hands were equally frenzied and impatient as he pushed the thin straps of her dress off her shoulders and let them fall to the crook of her arms.

He tore his lips from hers as the bodice of her outfit lowered with the straps, exposing her bare breasts to the cool air, which was quickly, shockingly replaced with the startling swoop of his hot, wet mouth on her flesh, then the scrape of his teeth across her taut, straining nipple. A full-body shudder rippled through her, and with a growl rumbling from the depths of Dylan's throat, he cupped the sides of her breasts in his hands and pushed them upward. His thumb and forefinger lightly pinched the sensitive peaks, sending a jolt of pure need straight to her clit, while his wicked tongue laved and flicked and curled around her nipple in a way that had her moaning shamelessly.

With his shirt undone and hanging open and his mouth busy sucking on her breasts, she slid a hand down his muscled abdomen and turned her attention to getting his belt unbuckled. She fumbled with his zipper until she managed to get it over the hard length of his erection, then slid her hand into his underwear and wrapped her fingers tight around his shaft. Brazen and bold, she squeezed and stroked him rhythmically, and he grunted in frustration and thrust along her palm while giving her nipple a firm, deliberate bite as he blatantly fucked the clasp of her hand.

After a moment, he straightened, flattened his hands on the wall behind her, and dropped his head back as he pushed harder against her hand. "Jesus fuck," he rasped gruffly, just as she felt a bead of pre-cum coat her fingers as she continued to tease and stroke every inch of his cock. And suddenly, she wanted to taste him, suck him, and blow his mind with pleasure.

Taking advantage of his moment of weakness, she dropped to her knees and had his pants and boxer briefs down to his thighs and her mouth enveloping his cock in the next few seconds. He sucked in a harsh, startled breath. His hand shot down to where she was kneeling and gathered her hair tight in his fingers, preventing her from taking him deeper.

Hands clenching his hard thighs, she cast her eyes up to his face. His features were tense, and she was certain he was going to pull her mouth away. But then he looked down at her through lust-filled eyes and groaned when she slid her soft tongue along the underside of his shaft, right against that pulsing vein leading up to the crown of his cock, deliberately teasing and tempting him. He tasted salty and male and so addicting she wanted more.

Apparently, he decided he wanted more, as well, because his dilated eyes went dark and hot as he held her head right where he needed her and languidly drove his hips forward, gradually giving her the last few inches of his cock until he finally hit the back of her throat and she had to force her jaw to relax. His breathing grew harsh, and with his unrelenting grip on her hair, he slowly withdrew, groaning like a dying man as she hollowed her cheeks and sucked all the way back to the swollen head. Then, as if he couldn't help himself, he did it again, this time thrusting his hips a little faster, sliding into her mouth a little harder, reaching a little deeper.

The muscles in his lower abdomen rippled, he gritted his teeth, and she felt his thighs tense beneath her palms, all signaling how close he was to coming. She was more than ready and willing to finish him off like this, but he abruptly pulled out of her mouth and instead hauled her back up to her feet. She barely had time to get her bearings before he was kissing her with so much passion and hunger and need it was almost overwhelming.

"We need a bed so I can fuck you properly," he said, his voice gravelly as he unexpectedly swept her up into his arms before she could respond to that statement. Not that she was about to argue with that delightful plan.

He carried her into one of the two bedrooms in the suite and kicked the door shut once they were inside. As soon as he put her down, their hands were everywhere on each other, removing the last of their clothing until everything was off but her heels. She reached down to unbuckle the straps around her ankles, but Dylan caught her wrist and stopped her.

"Leave them," he ordered in the hottest, sexiest voice she'd ever heard come out of him. "I want to fuck you with them on."

She straightened and raised a brow at his explicit request, which she hadn't expected from her analytical, sometimes nerdy best friend who always seemed so oblivious to her as an alluring woman. "You have a kinky shoe fetish I don't know about?"

"Maybe." The corner of his mouth quirked, even as his gaze raked down the length of her naked body, leaving fire and so much need in its wake. "Or a few fantasies I want to fulfill tonight that include you wrapping your gorgeous legs around me in those fuck-me heels. I did buy them, after all, so shouldn't I enjoy them?"

"Most definitely."

While he reached into the pocket of his duffle bag

to remove a few condoms and put them within reach, she moved up onto the mattress and settled against the pillows on her back, striking a seductive pose that left her breasts exposed to his captivating gaze, but bending a knee to keep her sex modestly covered so she didn't seem too eager and impatient, though she was feeling both of those things with him right now.

Standing at the foot of the bed, he rolled one of the condoms down his jutting shaft while shaking his head at her coy position. "Spread your legs nice and wide, sweetheart. I want to see what I'm about to taste and then fuck."

Those unrefined words sent a rush of excitement and anticipation through her, and she didn't hesitate to obey. Her thighs parted, fell open, revealing the most intimate part of herself to him. He hissed in a harsh sound as he looked down at her, his stare unabashedly focused on her neatly trimmed but very wet pussy.

"Jesus fucking Christ," he muttered beneath his breath as he moved up onto the bed. He made himself comfortable between her splayed thighs, his broad shoulders keeping them wide open while his hands gripped her hips to keep her still. "You're so damn beautiful," he added right before he put his hot mouth on her pussy and lavished her with immediate, thorough ecstasy.

Quick and dirty, he licked firmly along her sensitive flesh and, without hesitation, delved into the opening that seeped for his attention, making her whimper as he pushed shockingly deep. His tongue flicked across her distended clit with sinful, unapologetic precision before he grazed that taut nub with his teeth, then ruthlessly sucked it between his lips as if he owned her body and her pleasure.

Barely able to keep up with the assault on her senses, Serena's thighs trembled and her mind spun as he continued to devour her. This wasn't courtesy foreplay like she was used to with other men. No, this was a purposeful and determined seduction of her body, a blatant attempt to make her come hard and fast and without an ounce of reserve holding her back.

Oh, God, she was almost there . . .

He pushed two long fingers inside her, sliding them in and out, deliberately rubbing some reactive spot inside her sex that she'd never had the delight of discovering before, but the intensity of it wreaked havoc with her ability to do anything but grab handfuls of the comforter beside her and let the stunning, breath-stealing climax unravel her from the inside out. She jolted from the force of her release, cried out from the sheer bliss of all that heat and sensation spilling through her veins, and tingled from head to toe as she gradually came down from *the best* orgasmic high she'd ever had the satisfaction of experiencing.

Before the tremors in her body completely dissipated, Dylan reared up and quickly moved over her, all firm, toned muscle against her softer curves as he pinned her beneath him. She felt the tip of his shaft slide through her swollen, still pulsing sex as he lined himself up at her core. All ten of his fingers thrust into her hair to tip her head back, and all she was able to catch was the dark, feverish look in his eyes and the wild need etching his features as his lips landed on hers, unyielding and demanding. There was an undeniable desperation to his kiss, and she willingly opened to him, met the possessive thrust of tongue just as her body accepted the deeper, thicker invasion of his cock as he drove to the hilt inside her.

He swallowed her startled groan but didn't slow down. His tongue curled erotically around hers as his hips pumped erratically, almost frantically, as if he'd been pushed to the brink of control and there was no stopping the staggering surge of need overwhelming him. She understood the feeling, because she'd just experienced it herself . . . and it was about to consume her again.

Wrapping her arms around his neck, she bent her knees and secured her legs around his waist, making sure that he felt the scrape of her heels against his back to remind him she still had them on. His response was a feral growl and a quickening pace of his thrusts that had her arching beneath him, willing him deeper still.

He lifted his mouth from hers with a guttural gasp and stared down at her with passion and lust and so much more hazing his eyes. "Jesus, I'm going to fucking come. *Hard.*"

And then he did, tossing his head back and grinding against her with just the right pressure and friction to send her right over the edge with him.

When Dylan's body stopped convulsing and he seemed completely spent, he dropped on top of her, and she welcomed his weight as equally as she welcomed the happiness and contentment settling inside her. The kind that she'd been waiting years to feel with the one and only man she'd ever really wanted.

Tonight, the physical pleasure of being with Dylan had been more than she'd ever imagined or fantasized about. But it was the emotional connection that had hope blossoming in her heart and a soft smile on her face. She'd felt the shift between them, had seen not only the way he looked at her but the emotional reaction to his body inside hers while giving her the greatest pleasure imaginable, and it was more than enough to know that tonight changed everything between them in the best way possible.

She had no idea what it meant for them as a couple going forward, but they had plenty of time to figure it all out in the morning.

✧ ✧ ✧

OH, SHIT, WHAT have I done?

That was the immediate thought that entered Dylan's mind when he slowly blinked his eyes open the following morning and found Serena lying in his hotel room bed next to him, already awake as they lay facing one another. The misty look in her beautiful eyes and the soft, hopeful smile on her lips sent an initial surge of panic through him that was followed very closely by a strangling fear. One that made him realize that he might have, quite possibly, fucked up big-time, all because he hadn't been able to keep his dick in his pants when it came to *his best friend.*

Resisting Serena last night had been impossible, and he couldn't even say he'd been drunk or blame his behavior on an alcohol-induced haze. The unvarnished truth was, he'd wanted her badly, and the kiss she'd instigated out in the hallway had fueled that spark of desire he'd tried for years to ignore, and once he'd gotten a taste of how sweet and hot and sensual she was, he'd been like an addict who craved the entire feast. And Jesus Christ, he'd been absolutely gluttonous, because once he'd fucked her the first time, it hadn't been enough and he'd taken her twice more before they'd finally fallen asleep. He'd been selfish and stupid and so fucking greedy with her.

He'd always known mixing friendship and sex with

someone like Serena—who didn't sleep around casually and was looking for her forever guy—was the worst possible idea. She wanted and needed certain things in her life, in a relationship, to be exact, and he didn't do romance or commitment or emotional attachments with women for a reason. It just wasn't a part of his DNA, and he was practical and realistic enough to accept that truth about himself.

The last thing he ever wanted to do was give Serena the wrong impression about them as a couple, or any false hopes. He was well aware of her deeper feelings for him, and losing her as a best friend over sex would fucking slay him, which meant last night had to be a one-time, never-to-be-repeated deal. He also had to find a way, and quickly, to right what he'd made very wrong.

She bit her bottom lip as her gaze met and held his, suddenly looking nervous as she spoke. "Dylan . . . about last night . . ."

"It was a mistake," he blurted out before she finished, because he was desperate to keep their friendship intact, though judging by the hurt that flashed in her eyes, his choice of words had been shitty ones, which seemed par for the course for him this weekend.

"I'm sorry," he said, more gently this time as he got out of bed and put his pants on in an attempt to put things back to normal, if that was even possible. "Last night shouldn't have happened. I never would have slept with you if I'd been in my right mind."

He inwardly cringed as soon as the insulting sentence was out and he saw her crushed expression. *Oh, yeah, like that statement was any better, asshole.*

Christ, he sucked at eloquent words and articulating himself when it came to this sentimental crap, which only reinforced one of the reasons he found relationships so difficult. It was so much easier for him to translate code and to decipher HTML tags than it was for him to relate emotionally to a woman. Apparently, that included his best friend.

He exhaled a deep breath, knowing anything else he said would probably just make things worse, so he kept his next question as simple as possible. "We're good, right?"

Averting her gaze, she sat up on the bed, holding the covers to her chest like a shield, as if she was trying to protect her body and her heart from any more damage he might inflict. "Yeah. Sure," she replied, a forced sound to her voice. "We're good."

"Okay," he said, but as he headed into the adjoining bathroom, he had a sinking feeling that their friendship would never be the same.

AN AMAZING NIGHT with Dylan, followed by his morning-after rejection, devastated Serena. He'd shattered her heart into a thousand pieces, and it hurt to breathe. Not to mention the embarrassment and humiliation she'd felt after baring herself, physically and emotionally, to the one person she'd trusted the most.

The most awful, painful part of it all? She'd honestly had no idea what heartbreak really felt like until that moment, because her feelings for Dylan were by far the strongest she'd ever felt for any man.

As she heard the shower in the bathroom turn on, Serena ran her fingers through her disheveled hair and forced herself to get out of the bed and start moving, so she'd be gone before he came back out, because there was nothing left for them to say and it would undoubtedly be awkward for both of them. But as she slipped into the dress she'd worn last night, there was only one thought that kept replaying through her mind . . . *How could she have been so wrong about his feelings for her?*

Clearly, she'd misinterpreted the entire night and she felt foolish and stupid for believing he'd ever see her as anything more than a best friend, or that a night of sex with her would change the way he saw her. His words, *it was a mistake*, had made her stomach roll, but had also been the wake-up call she apparently needed to realize that she'd been deluding herself, holding on to hope she hadn't even realized she'd had, that someday he'd admit his true feelings for her.

So, she was forced to swallow her hurt and her pride and finally accept that Dylan was never going to fall in love with her and it was useless to wait or hope. There was truly only one thing left she could do, and that was to lock up her hopes, dreams, and unrequited feelings for Dylan in the furthest reaches of her heart and keep searching for the one guy who would love and appreciate her and give her all the things that Dylan never would.

Chapter Eight

THE KNOCK ON Serena's apartment door signaled the arrival of her date, a new guy she'd been seeing for the past two weeks who she'd invited to join her for Trivia Night at the local pub . . . mostly because she wasn't ready to deal with Dylan alone after the disastrous way things had ended between them in Vegas over three weeks ago. Her heart was still feeling battered and bruised, and she was trying to get on with her life now that she knew her feelings for Dylan would never be reciprocated.

They'd agreed that they were "fine," but the truth was, Serena hadn't been the same since then, and neither had their friendship, and for the first time in the year and a half that they'd been attending the monthly game night together as trivia partners, she wasn't going with Dylan. Instead, she was taking a date.

As for the man she was about to greet on her doorstep who'd be accompanying her, she'd known

Grant for a while. He worked part-time as a barista at a nearby coffee shop where she stopped in the mornings for her cup of coffee on her way to work, and he'd always greeted her with a charming smile and a flirty comment. He'd finally gotten up the nerve to ask her out, and how was a girl able to resist the kind of cute message he'd written on her paper cup that was the only thing that had made her truly smile since that fateful night with Dylan?

In black marker, his neat handwriting had said, *If you're single, I'm available*, followed by his cell phone number. Making the decision to text Grant later that evening hadn't been an easy one, but with her vow to start fresh and with an open mind about men other than Dylan, she'd started a conversation with Grant, and over the course of the past few weeks, she'd grown to really like him and enjoy his company.

He was intelligent and a bit nerdy, which she found endearing, even if those traits did remind her of Dylan. He was also very motivated when it came to what he wanted in life and for his future. Currently, he was working as a barista in the mornings while in the afternoons and evenings, he focused on finishing up the dissertation for his master's degree in psychology. His weekends were spent at a nonprofit mental health clinic as a social worker. He didn't have much free time in his schedule, but when he did, like tonight, he was more than willing to spend it with her.

Grant was respectful, easygoing with a great sense of humor, attentive and affectionate when they were together, and came from a close-knit family with a dozen nieces and nephews he seemed to adore. So far, there hadn't been any huge warning signs flashing at her, and she was determined to stay positive and enjoy her evening out with him at the pub.

She opened the door and Grant greeted her with a smile and a bouquet of pretty daisies. He was a good-looking guy with dark brown, neatly trimmed hair and light blue eyes that sparkled behind the black-rimmed glasses he wore. He was a few inches shorter than Dylan, and much leaner, his chest not as defined or broad . . . and God, she had to stop making comparisons between the two because there was no future with Dylan, so it no longer mattered how attractive he'd always been to her.

Once Grant stepped inside her apartment, he held the flowers out to her. "I saw these and thought of you."

She took the lovely blooms from him, easily adding *considerate* to his list of attributes. "Thank you. They're beautiful."

"No, *you're* the beautiful one," he said, brushing a soft, sweet kiss against her lips, with no expectation of anything more than that chaste peck—because he was a gentleman, she told herself.

There was no zing or spark or wild urge to tear Grant's clothes off and jump his bones. And yes, they'd already kissed with tongue, which had been nice and pleasant enough, but lacked the crazy hot chemistry she'd had with Dylan in Vegas, and she'd pretty much resigned herself to the fact that she might not ever find that kind of intense passion again. It was a sad realization, but an honest one, too.

She went to the kitchen and put the daisies in a vase with water so they wouldn't wilt. Once that was done, she turned back to face Grant, who was standing a few feet away, his hands in the front pockets of his khaki pants, waiting patiently for her to finish.

"Ready to go?" he asked. "I want to make sure we're not late for the start of the game."

And punctual. Serena gave her date a nod as she picked up her purse from the counter. She was about as ready to finally face Dylan as she'd ever be.

THREE FUCKING *AGONIZING* weeks, Dylan thought as his fingers tightened around the cold bottle of beer the bartender at the pub had just slid across the counter to him. That's how long it had been since he'd seen or spoken to Serena, when they'd previously never gone more than a few days without some kind of contact, even after an argument.

But this separation between them hadn't been for a lack of trying on his end. His calls went straight through to voicemail, and because it irritated the hell out of him that Serena didn't pick up, he never left a message. He'd texted her a few times, only to get a short, to-the-point answer. He hated how impersonal her responses had become, how distant *they'd* become.

He'd sent the latest text a few days ago in hopes that getting back to their normal routine would finally put their friendship on the right track again. *What time should I pick you up for trivia night?* he'd asked. Since they'd always driven together and were game partners for the once-a-month event, it was a logical assumption and a great way to break the ice. Or so he thought.

Waiting for her response had been excruciating, and her reply made him feel as though he'd been gut punched. *No need. I have a date and he's taking me.*

What. The. Fuck. That had been his immediate internal reaction. She was bringing a goddamn date when trivia night had always been *their* thing. Together, as a team, they usually kicked everyone else's ass and were the current reigning champs. Now, they'd be competing against one another.

Jesus. Everything that was comfortable and routine and familiar with Serena had pretty much gone to shit since he'd taken her to bed and he was all out of sorts because of it. He'd tried to do the right thing the morning after their night together, but there was no denying that he'd fucked everything up and his most deep-seated fears were coming true, that crossing those lines with Serena had changed the whole dynamic of their relationship.

Nothing was the same between them, and the worst part was, he missed his best friend like crazy and felt as though a crucial part of himself had been severed, and he had no clue what to do to fix the damage he'd done. The loss ate at him, consumed him, and made him prickly and moody in general.

Out of the corner of his eye, Dylan saw someone enter the establishment and glanced toward the entrance to the pub, hoping to see Serena, even if she was with another man. Instead, Eric strolled in, spotted him sitting at the bar, and headed his way, passing the other customers gathering around to sign up for the game.

"I can't believe you talked me into doing this," Eric said as he slid into the chair beside Dylan's. "Just as full disclosure, I fucking suck at trivia games."

"You can just sit there and look pretty," Dylan said, motioning for the bartender to bring Eric a beer, too. "I don't need your brain, just your presence. I can't play without a partner, and since Serena is bringing someone else, I had to settle for you because you were the only person available tonight."

"Wow, that kind of hurts my feelings," Eric joked as he took a drink of the beer that had just been delivered. "I take it you and Serena haven't kissed and made up yet after what happened in Vegas?"

"No," he snapped irritably, watching as a few more customers walked into the pub and stopped at the sign-up table. "I haven't seen her in three fucking weeks. She hasn't returned my calls and has pretty much made me persona non grata."

"That's what you get for messing around with your best friend. You had to have known it wouldn't end well." Eric shook his head, as if Dylan was an idiot for sticking his dick where it didn't belong, and Dylan couldn't disagree. "Those kinds of things never end well, unless the one-night stand rules are established right up front. If not, women start expecting certain things . . . like hearts and flowers and a whole lot of attention."

"Is that how it is between you and Chelsea?" Dylan asked curiously. The two had hit it off well in Vegas, and he had no idea if they'd dated since.

"Actually, no." Eric shrugged casually, seemingly fine with that status quo. "Chelsea and I went into that night with the understanding that it was a one-time hookup, so no awkward morning after for us. Didn't you do the same with Serena?"

Dylan shook his head, unable to imagine suggesting a one-night stand with Serena. "She's not a friends-with-benefits kind of woman."

Eric smirked at him. "Yet you enjoyed some pretty major benefits with your best friend."

Dylan opened his mouth to tell Eric to fuck off, even if it was the truth, then promptly snapped it shut again when he saw Serena walk into the bar, looking so stunningly beautiful his heart hammered in his chest and his stomach swirled as if a dozen butterflies had taken flight inside. *What the hell was up with that?*

His gaze drank her up as though he'd been dying of thirst, taking in all that soft blonde hair he loved, her pretty face and bright eyes, and the demure dress that was a far cry from the racy one she'd worn in Vegas, but was so *her*. This was his girl, his best friend, and for a moment everything was right in his world.

Then he saw her holding hands with the guy she was with, and smiling at her date in the same way she used to smile at *him*, and that sensation in his belly immediately soured. They stopped at the table to sign up for the game, then Serena glanced around the bar area until she found him sitting at the bar with Eric.

She said something to her date, he nodded, and then they started walking in his direction. Dylan searched Serena's features as they approached, desperate to see that brilliant sparkle in her eyes when she looked at him or that sweet smile that always made him feel like he was her knight in shining armor, but by the time the two of them reached the bar, all Dylan saw was a woman who was distant and guarded, her expression cool and unreadable.

"Hey, guys," she said, her polite tone grating on Dylan's nerves. "I just wanted to come over and say hi before the game started and introduce you to my date." She proceeded to acquaint Eric with the guy named Grant, they shook hands, then she turned to Dylan. "And this is Dylan, a childhood friend of mine," she said, delegating him to nothing more than someone she'd grown up with, instead of the guy who knew her deepest secrets and fears because he'd *always* been there for her.

"It's nice to meet you both," Grant said, adjusting the black-rimmed glasses on the bridge of his nose.

Eric studied Grant intently. "Do I know you from somewhere? You look really familiar."

"Have you ever been to the Espresso Cup?" Grant asked. When Eric nodded, he continued. "That's probably where you've seen me. I work as a barista there, usually the morning shift during the week."

A barista? Really? Dylan decided his nickname was going to be Coffee Bean Guy, and tried to hide the smirk threatening to appear, but Serena knew him too well and caught that smug curve to his mouth.

She looped her arm through Grant's in full support and smiled up at him. "He's also finishing up his dissertation for his master's degree in psychology, and works at a nonprofit mental health clinic on the weekends."

Okay, yeah, that was an impressive resume, Dylan had to admit, which meant Grant most likely had quite the repertoire stored up for trivia. "Did Serena tell you that she and I have been the reigning trivia champions for the past three months?"

Grant shook his head, not bothered by the fact that Dylan had just insinuated that he and Serena were closer than she'd indicated during their introduction. "No, she didn't mention that. Probably because she didn't want me to feel pressured to win tonight's game."

Serena narrowed her gaze at Dylan, obviously seeing right through his ruse. "I didn't tell him because it doesn't matter," she said succinctly. "Tonight is a clean slate, so it's anybody's game."

"Oooh, burn," Eric muttered beside Dylan.

Grant settled his hand over the one Serena had on his arm, the gesture familiar and intimate. "Considering the two of you are opponents tonight with different partners, it should make for an interesting game."

"Yes, it should," Dylan agreed. "May the best man win."

Serena rolled her eyes, as if to say, *Really? You're going to make this a competition because you think you're the better man?*

Why, yes, yes he was.

The person in charge of the evening's event made the announcement for everyone to sit at their designated table so the game could start, which put Dylan across the room from Serena and Coffee Bean Guy. The rules were set. The game consisted of a total of fifty questions. The first team to buzz in with the correct answer won a point, and the points were then tallied at the end of the game to determine the winning team.

While the emcee gathered the questions for the first round, Eric glanced at Dylan, an amused smile on his lips. "So, just pointing out that you might have been a bit on the aggressive side with that last 'may the best man win' challenge you issued to Grant."

Dylan glared at Eric. "Yeah, well, I don't like him." Which seemed to be a recurring theme for him with the men Serena had dated lately.

Eric's laugh was filled with humor. "He seems like a perfectly nice guy. Besides, you don't know him well enough to make that judgment call, unless it's based on your feelings for Serena, which, in that case, I completely understand why you wouldn't like him."

"What's that supposed to mean?" Dylan asked, fiddling with the buzzer on the table.

"That no matter what kind of guy she dates, he's never going to be good enough, because you want Serena for yourself."

Dylan *did* want her for himself. Oh, God, he really did. But when it came to Serena, his wants and desires were selfish ones because he just couldn't give her the things she needed and deserved, and the chance to have the kind of marriage and family she longed for was the one thing he'd never take away from her.

A loud buzzing snapped Dylan back to the present, along with Coffee Bean Guy's voice calling out, "Big toe!" and the emcee awarding him the point for answering correctly.

"Big toe?" he asked Eric, annoyed with himself for allowing thoughts of Serena to divert his attention from the game. "What the hell was the question?"

"In the human body, what is the hallux?" Eric repeated, then gave Dylan a pointed look. "I had no idea, but I thought you said you were good at this."

"I *am* good at this," Dylan argued, watching as Serena gave Grant a high five, which was something *they'd* always done. "I knew that answer."

"Well, clearly you didn't win the point," Eric drawled.

Dylan swallowed a not-so-nice response and positioned his hand right above the red plastic buzzer, watching as Coffee Bean Guy said something to make Serena laugh. He heard the sweet, affectionate sound from across the room and a shaft of white-hot jealousy sliced right through him.

Another loud buzz rang out, and a woman yelled, "Millennium Falcon!"

"Fuck," Dylan swore beneath his breath, and glanced at Eric, who was trying to hold back laughter. "I take it the question was, 'What is the name of Han Solo's ship'?"

"Yep," he confirmed with a nod. "You're kind of late on the trigger though."

"Whatever." Dylan gave his head a hard shake to completely clear it from all distractions and focused on the next round.

The guy holding the microphone cleared his throat before asking, "In what year was the fugitive slave law—"

Buzz! The question wasn't even finished and Serena shouted out, "Eighteen fifty!"

"That's right," the emcee said, impressed that she'd guessed accurately. "Eighteen fifty was the year the fugitive slave law was passed."

Dylan groaned as she was awarded another point and did that cute, excited shimmy thing in her chair that she'd always done with him when they won a round. He'd always sucked at learning history, while Serena had minored in the subject in college. What his nerdy brain hadn't retained from school, her more refined one had, which was why they'd always made such a great trivia duo. Tonight, she had a partner who was holding his own, and Dylan had a teammate who didn't seem to know shit, or didn't care if he won. The odds were not in Dylan's favor.

Eric chuckled. "You are so off your game tonight."

"Yeah, well, that's all about to change," Dylan said, his tone serious as he cracked his knuckles and blocked out everything but the questions that were being asked. No way was he going to let team Coffee Bean walk away victorious tonight.

For the next hour, teams battled it out. With each round, the questions became more difficult and other pairs started falling so far behind on points that the emcee dropped them out of the game, until it was just Dylan and Grant suddenly having a dick-measuring contest with the two of them trying to out-trivia one another, while Serena watched the ridiculous rivalry unfold, and Eric finished off his third beer. Dylan knew he was being a chest-pounding, alpha asshole, trying to one-up her date. And he didn't care.

"Last question coming up," the emcee announced, pulling a card with the final trivia of the night. "We've got two teams left battling it out for the win. Who is going to be this month's champion and walk away with bragging rights and a fifty-dollar gift certificate to enjoy dinner and drinks here at the pub?"

"I am," Dylan muttered, adrenaline pumping through his veins as he positioned his hand above the buzzer once more.

Across the bar, Grant did the same, both of them poised and ready.

"What type of charge does a neutron carry?" the emcee asked.

The answer to the chemistry question was a no-brainer for Dylan, and he slammed his hand down on the button, mere seconds *after* Grant hit his. The guy with the microphone turned toward Serena's date to hear his answer, while Dylan prepared himself for defeat.

"A negative charge," Grant said confidently.

"Nooo," the emcee said, as shocked as the rest of the players watching the end to the game. "That is not the correct answer, which gives your opponent the chance to steal the final point and win tonight's game if his response is accurate."

All eyes turned to Dylan in anticipation, but the only ones he connected with were Serena's. For a moment, all those walls she'd recently erected between them were down, giving him a glimpse of the woman who'd once desired him and made him feel whole and complete when he was with her. Until she glanced away, reminding him that he'd royally fucked up the best part of his life.

Trying to ignore the searing pain in his chest, he glanced at the emcee and stated the correct answer to the question. "Neutrons are particles with no charge."

"'No charge' is accurate, which makes your team tonight's winners!"

Eric laughed while most of the players cheered and clapped. "I'll be damned, we won."

Dylan shot him a mocking look. "Just for the record, *you* didn't win jack."

"Okay, that's a fair point," Eric conceded, and slapped Dylan on the back. "The least I can do is buy you a drink to commemorate the occasion."

They headed over to the bar, but Dylan also watched Serena and her date, who weren't sticking around for the celebratory festivities and were getting ready to leave for the evening. As Eric pushed a shot of high-end tequila in front of him, Dylan came to a bitter realization.

He might have won the trivia bragging rights for a month, but Grant was going home with the girl, and Dylan wished it was him instead.

Chapter Nine

DYLAN STARED AT his computer screen, unable to believe that after weeks of frustration, troubleshooting, and setbacks on the code for the Boyfriend Experience app, it was finally working without any issues. All system files and links checked out, and now it was just a matter of getting the app beta tested before releasing it to the public.

He sat back in his office chair and grinned to himself. "Holy shit, I finally figured it out," he said, both exhilarated and relieved that the codes and interface were free of bugs and glitches and the app was working smoothly and as it should.

"Figured out what, boss?" Owen, the marketing manager at Stone Media, asked as he walked into Dylan's office.

"The issue on the Boyfriend Experience app that's been making me crazy the past few weeks," Dylan said, crossing his hands behind his head as he leaned back farther in his leather chair. "The problem has been identified and fixed, and the app itself is ready to rock and roll."

"Oh, cool." All business, Owen's tone lacked the level of enthusiasm Dylan was hoping for as he set a few sheets of paper on Dylan's desk. "Here's the printout of the specs you wanted for the initial framework and design for the Sapphire Casino and Hotel prototype app. I just wanted to make sure you had everything to review before I left for the evening."

"Yeah, thanks. I appreciate it." Dylan glanced over the computer-generated wireframe diagram, then looked at Owen again. "We'll go over all this in tomorrow morning's staff meeting. Also, let's talk about getting the beta testing rolling on the Boyfriend Experience app and set up a firm launch date."

"Will do." Owen headed out of his office with a wave. "I'll see you in the morning, boss."

Alone again, and with no one around to share in Dylan's initial excitement over the Boyfriend Experience app, his own enthusiasm waned and he couldn't help but feel a sense of gnawing emptiness inside. It wasn't difficult to pinpoint why he felt that way, considering it had all started when Serena stopped being his go-to person for just about everything. The separation was her doing, not his, but it had happened nonetheless, and not having his best friend around anymore royally sucked.

Normally, she'd be the first person he'd call to tell about the app, especially considering the two of them had created the concept together one night when she'd ended up on his doorstep after one of her dates from hell. At first, the suggestion had been nothing more than a joke, but by the end of that night and after a carton of Ben & Jerry's, it had become a fully formed idea they both knew would appeal to women who wanted or needed a temporary date or boyfriend for personal or business reasons.

So, really, while Serena had been the inspiration behind the app's purpose, it had been both of their brainchild, and up until Vegas, he'd shared the entire step-by-step process with her. The fact that he couldn't do that now was, well, depressing as hell.

Then again, why *couldn't* he tell her, he wondered as he drummed his fingers on the surface of his desk, an idea forming in his mind. She might not pick up his phone calls, but if he just showed up at her door on a Wednesday evening, would she really shut it in his face or turn him away? Probably not. He'd given her time and space, and goddamnit, he wanted his best friend back.

Decision made, he shut down his computer, locked up the office, and drove to Serena's apartment complex. As he pulled into one of the nearby guest parking spots, he caught Grant leaving her place, and

Dylan turned off his engine so he could cloak himself in the darkness until Coffee Bean Guy was gone.

After stepping onto her small front porch, Grant turned back to Serena and went in for a kiss. She didn't refuse him, and Dylan felt his stomach muscles cramp in pure jealousy. He could still remember what those plush lips felt like beneath his, how sweet she tasted, and the soft, arousing noises she made as he'd deepened the kiss and she melted against him. And now, it was pure fucking torture to watch another man take those liberties when there wasn't a damn thing Dylan could do about it.

He wasn't there to cause trouble with Coffee Bean Guy, but he'd be lying if he said he didn't want Serena for himself. He did. So badly, he ached with a searing need that was difficult to ignore. But tonight was about reestablishing their friendship, and not staking a claim, and he exhaled a deep breath and kept reminding himself of that fact.

As soon as Grant drove out of the complex, Dylan made his way up to Serena's door and knocked. It opened a few seconds later.

"Hey, did you forget something . . ." Her words trailed off and the lighthearted smile on Serena's face turned into a frown. "Oh. I was expecting Grant."

He pushed his hands into the front pockets of his jeans and gave her one of those dimpled grins that usually softened her right up. "Well, you would have known it was me if you'd looked through the peephole," he joked.

She wasn't amused. She crossed her arms over her chest, and he recognized it for the emotionally defensive, protective gesture it was. "What do you want, Dylan?" she asked, her voice almost sounding vulnerable. As if she was fighting her feelings for him, trying to hold back, and it gave him a sliver of hope. "I have papers to grade tonight."

Ouch. That hurt. She could spend time with Grant with those papers waiting to be graded, but now Dylan was the equivalent of chopped liver? Yeah, that definitely stung.

"Can I come in?" he asked.

Her eyes swam with the hurt he'd inflicted on her over a month ago, even though he'd apologized for what had happened that night in Vegas, for letting his own desire for her shatter the control he'd spent his adult years keeping in check around her. But Jesus, the want and need were still there simmering beneath the surface, possibly even stronger than before. And he had no clue what to do with all the weird feelings swirling inside him.

"Please?" His own voice was low, almost a bit pleading, because he didn't think he could bear to hear her say no to him. "It'll just be for a few minutes."

She stood firm for a few more seconds, and then her stiff shoulders and cautious body language eased as she stepped aside and widened the door for him to enter. He did, gratefully, and didn't stop until they were in her living room and he was facing her. She was dressed for an evening in, wearing a comfortable pair of drawstring sweatpants with a simple T-shirt and her hair piled up on her head. She'd stuck a pencil through the mass to hold it in place, and all he could think was that her outfit was not one meant for seduction, and she'd probably sent Grant on his way without him getting lucky for the night.

And yeah, that possibility pleased Dylan immensely.

Serena stared at him expectantly, and he cleared his throat and rerouted his thoughts to the reason he was there.

"The Boyfriend Experience app is done," he told her, retrieving his cell phone from his back pocket to show her the final interface. "It took me forever to locate that last glitch, but I finally fixed it and now we're getting ready to push the app into beta testing. I wanted you to know, since this was your idea as much as mine."

At that news, her eyes lit up with the excitement he'd been craving, and his heart raced when he saw glimpses of Serena, the woman who'd always been his best friend. The one person he'd shared everything with, who made him whole and complete, and it felt so fucking good to see that lighthearted, joyful girl reappear in front of him again when he thought he might have lost her for good.

Optimism filled Dylan as he went through the app with Serena, covering all the new features and showing her how it all worked and integrated. He loved her enthusiasm as she asked questions, moving closer and closer to his side to see his phone screen more clearly. When he was done with the demonstration, she looked up at him with an unguarded, genuinely happy smile that hit him like pure sunshine that chased away the cloud of gloom that had been hovering over him for weeks.

Of its own accord, his gaze lowered to her mouth, and suddenly, seemingly out of nowhere, everything shifted and changed between them, and it was as though both of them had been transported back to that night in Vegas, to the part where they'd surrendered to the kind of intense passion and desire he'd never experienced with any other woman.

The thick, undeniable awareness seemed to draw them together like a magnet. Her lips parted as she stared into his eyes as if hypnotized by the irresistible pull between them, her breathing slowing, deepening, while her irises darkened to midnight blue.

Temptation beckoned to him. "Serena," he whispered, that ache in his chest spreading to every limb in his body, making him weak with longing.

The guttural, almost helpless tone to his voice seemed to penetrate her haze, and she gave her head a stern shake as though to clear it, then took a safe step back as if she didn't trust him, or even herself.

She nervously wiped her hands down the front of her sweatpants and tried to gather her composure, as well as put up that goddamn wall between them again. "I'm really glad you figured out the problem with the app," she said, as if she was talking to a business associate instead of a guy she'd known her entire life. "It's great, by the way. If I was single, I'd use it."

The bland, almost aloof tone of her voice scraped along his nerves. Oh, yeah, she was totally scrambling to get her emotions back under control, while he wanted to obliterate her suddenly cool, detached demeanor.

"What do you mean, if you were single?"

She shrugged. "Well, I'm dating someone, as you already know."

"Oh, you mean Coffee Bean Guy?"

She blinked in startled surprise at the nickname he'd given her current beau, but didn't crack a smile like she normally would have. "Yeah, that would be him. His name is Grant, by the way."

"I know what his name is, I just prefer Coffee Bean Guy." It was fitting, considering he was a barista at an espresso place. "Is it serious with him?"

The question came out before he could stop it, but he had to know, because the thought of some other man completely and totally replacing him in Serena's life made Dylan more than a little insane. Why he hadn't realized that before now was beyond him. That her getting everything she wanted, a man with whom she could have everything she desired, meant he would lose the bond he had with her.

Her chin lifted, and her eyes sparked with stubborn defiance. "It's serious enough. Not that it should make any difference to you."

But it *did* make a difference. More than it should and in ways he didn't even know how to express because he wasn't a guy who'd ever used those flowery, emotional words that females always seemed to want and need to hear. But this conversation, and Serena's insinuation that things were perfectly awesome and amazing with Grant, was chafing him raw. It was also stirring up some major possessiveness that was provoking him to do stupid shit.

Like ask this next question . . . "Have you had sex with him yet?"

She sucked in an affronted breath, which was ridiculous because she never used to have an issue discussing those things with him. "That's none of your business."

That certainly wasn't a yes, and her big, round, blue eyes told him that she was getting ready to fib if she needed to. He took a slow, purposeful step toward her, and instead of annoyance or anger, he saw her eyes flare with desire, which clearly wasn't for Coffee Bean Guy because he was nowhere in sight.

"Have you had sex with him yet?" Dylan asked, softer now, but no less challenging as he took the final step that put him toe-to-toe with her.

She tipped her head back to look up at him. "It's none of your business," she reiterated, her voice wavering, while her gaze shimmered with an arousing heat that provided him with the truth that he sought.

He smiled triumphantly. "You haven't slept with him yet."

She didn't back off or admit defeat. "How do you know that?"

He let his gaze drift down, taking in the hard nipples poking against her T-shirt . . . the pulse beating wildly at the base of her throat . . . her flushed face . . . and those eyes that were like a window into her soul and told him everything he needed to know.

It also made his answer to her question incredibly easy to deliver. "Because if you were sleeping with Grant, you wouldn't be looking at me like you want me to fuck you again."

She scoffed and jabbed him in the chest with her index finger. "You are so full of yourself, Dylan."

He arched a brow. "Am I? Really?" Before she realized his intent, he caught her face in his hands, holding her tight enough that she couldn't escape what was about to happen. "Then fucking prove it, Serena." *Resist this*, he thought as his mouth came down on hers. *Resist me.* And if she could do that, *then* he'd believe she truly didn't want him.

She gasped against his lips and her hands shot up, flattening defensively against his chest. As his fingers tightened on her jaw and his tongue swept demandingly inside her mouth, he braced himself for her to push him away. He felt a moment of pressure as the heels of her hands dug into his muscles, then seconds later, her fingers fisted in his T-shirt instead. She pulled him closer and moaned in pleasure, her entire body softening against his—right where she fucking belonged.

The kiss was hot, deep, and intense. Demanding and combustive, and Serena mewled seductively against his lips and arched into him, rubbing her pelvis against the thick length of his cock straining against the zipper of his jeans. Her uninhibited, greedy response gave him all the proof he required to know that she was *his*. Nobody else's, and God, he wanted it to stay that way forever.

He dropped one hand to the waistband of her sweats and tugged the tie loose enough that he could slide his hand inside her panties and between her legs, where she was already slick with desire. She shamelessly rocked against his fingers while he skimmed his lips along her jaw, then trailed them down the side of her neck with a light scrape of his teeth and puffs of hot, damp breath against her skin that made her shiver and another rush of moisture coat his hand.

He moved his mouth up to the shell of her ear as he glided his fingers against her swollen, needy clit. "Tell me, Serena," he rasped in a heated breath. "When *he* kisses you, do you get all hot and wet like you do for me?"

Her fingernails dug into his shoulders, and her hips arched against his hand. Closing her eyes, she shook her head as if she didn't want to answer his question or face the truth. "Dylan . . ."

He pushed two long fingers deep into her pussy, all the way to the second knuckle, making her cry out as he pumped them in and out, filling her, stretching her, and stroking those inner walls where she was the most sensitive. "Answer. Me." Each word came out as a gruff demand.

She shook her head, her breathing quickening, her body trembling as he kept her right on the edge, despite her trying to ride his hand to release. "No," she moaned desperately.

He wasn't letting her off that easily. "No, what?" he growled, wanting to hear her say the words out loud. "Look at me when you answer." Because it was equally important for her to meet his gaze when she admitted the truth.

Her lids fluttered open, and her hands came up to cradle his face with excruciating gentleness as she stared into his eyes, baring herself to him. "No, Dylan. He doesn't make me hot and wet like you do. Nobody ever has. Not like this."

Her confession unlocked something inside of him. Something wild and untamed and beyond his control or comprehension. He grabbed the back of her neck with his free hand and claimed her mouth once again with his own, sliding his tongue as deep as his fingers thrusting between her thighs. His thumb worked her clit, giving her the pressure and friction she needed to send her soaring. Burying her face against his neck and hanging on to him for dear life, she cried out as her orgasm pulsed through her and had his dick throbbing for its own release.

A minute or so later, when he knew she had her bearings back and could think clearly, he withdrew his fingers and reached for the hem of her T-shirt, yanking it up and off her in one smooth move.

"Too many fucking clothes," he muttered, and she

must have agreed because she eagerly helped him out of his, too, until they were both standing in her living room naked.

She pressed her warm, lush body against his and reached between them to stroke his cock, nice and tight and slow as she placed soft kisses on his jaw, his neck, her tongue darting out to taste his salty skin. Precum was already seeping from the tip, and considering how aroused he was, Dylan knew it would only take a few strokes of a hand job from her to make him come, and he wanted to be deep inside her when that happened.

And then he realized he didn't have any protection with him, because there was no way he would have ever predicted that this evening would end with sex. "Oh, fuck," he said beneath his breath, startling her enough that she moved her head back to look into his eyes. He squeezed his own shut, because he couldn't think straight when she was sliding his dick through her fist.

"I don't have a condom with me," he said, his voice hoarse with disappointment.

"You don't need one." She pressed another light kiss to his jaw, gave his shaft another firm squeeze. "I'm on birth control, and I'm good if you are."

He knew what she was saying, and he opened his eyes, held her gaze, and gave her the reassurance she deserved. "I'm clean." He'd never had sex without a condom, and there had been no issues during his last physical and blood test.

"I trust you," she said.

Those words . . . they meant *everything* to him. *She* meant everything to him. "Bedroom?" he suggested.

Her mouth tipped up in a playful smile that made his heart feel as though it flipped over in his chest. "No. How about right here," she said, and pushed him backwards until his legs hit the edge of the couch and he had no other option but to sit.

She was gloriously, beautifully naked, and he drank in the soft, lush curves of her body as she reached up and pulled the pencil from her upswept hair. A low groan of approval rumbled in his chest as he watched in fascination as those silky strands tumbled down around her shoulders. She closed the distance between them, straddled his lap, and he held his cock upright as she slowly, seductively, lowered herself on him. He sank inside her, inch by decadent inch, until they were joined completely and he was buried to the hilt.

The feel of her body clasping his with nothing separating them was indescribable and sublime. A delightful sigh slipped past her lips, and she braced her hands on his shoulders, tipped her head back, and rolled her hips against his, fucking him at her own leisure. He filled his hands with her full breasts, squeezing the firm flesh, and when that was no longer enough for him, he flattened one of his palms in the middle of Serena's back and drew her body closer so he could lower his head and circle her stiff nipples with his tongue.

He sucked those tight, puckered tips, pinched them, bit them until they were rock hard and rosy. Each increasing level of pleasurable pain had her gasping and grinding against him harder, faster, taking him deeper, and driving them both toward release. Grabbing her waist, he brought Serena down on his cock as he thrust upward, pumping his hips and taking control. He heard her cry out as she clenched around his shaft, milking him as his balls tightened and his own orgasm surged through him in hot, pulsing jets. Aftershocks rattled through both of them, until they were too exhausted to move.

With his cock deep inside Serena and their bodies still joined, and her cuddled so warm and perfectly against his chest, the only thought that filled Dylan's head was that *she's mine. She's all fucking mine.*

Chapter Ten

S ERENA WOKE UP to the smell of coffee and the sound of Dylan rattling around in her kitchen. She should have been elated after her night with him, but the truth was, in the light of day, a huge dose of reality was crashing over her and chasing away her post-orgasmic bliss. Her chest hurt at the knowledge at what she had to do to protect her emotions, because she couldn't keep doing *this* with Dylan.

Without question, sex with Dylan was ah-ma-zing. The best she'd ever had, and she was certain it would be a very long time, if ever, before she found the kind of heat and connection with another man that she shared with Dylan. However, she didn't want to be just fuck buddies with him, or a convenient booty call to scratch an itch, because as much as she knew he cared about her, she wanted, and needed, his love. There was no in-between for her, and never had been. And every time she gave him the most intimate part of her, knowing he'd never return those deeper emotions she craved from him because he didn't believe himself capable, made her heart break a little more.

With Dylan, she was open and vulnerable, and in order to save her heart from shattering irreparably, she was going to have to make one of the most difficult decisions she'd ever had to make. And hope she survived the pain of losing the one man who meant everything to her.

Unfortunately, she envisioned a lot of Ben & Jerry's and Hallmark movies in her near future to distract her from her pain and misery, but no one to share them with.

Dreading the conversation she was about to have with him, she forced herself out of the warm bed, her body sore after the numerous times Dylan had taken her during the course of the night. Hard and deep. Gentle and slow. And every way in between. He'd been greedy and insatiable, yet generous with her pleasure, and she'd bet every penny in her savings account that their night together meant more to him than just sex. She was also smart enough to know that he didn't believe in the forever, soul-mate kind of love like she did, and she couldn't force him to be the kind of man she needed in her life. The man she knew he could be, if he would just believe in himself. Believe in *her*.

And that meant she had to let him go, because it

hurt too much to have him in her life on a regular basis—being in love with him knowing he'd never return her feelings in that way. She just couldn't do it anymore.

The thought caused a huge, aching lump to form in her throat as she went into the bathroom. After a quick washup and brushing her disheveled hair, Serena put on a clean pair of sweats and T-shirt, then headed out to the kitchen. Dylan was standing at the counter, his naked back to her since he was only wearing a pair of jeans that rode very low on his hips.

The muscles across his shoulders bunched as he stirred what looked like pancake batter in a bowl, judging by the ingredients still left out around him. His hair was tousled around his head, and knowing it was most likely the last time she'd be able to look at him like this, she let her gaze trail down his back to the sexy divots right above his firm buttocks. This scene was a familiar one, where Dylan would make her breakfast, her favorite chocolate chip pancakes, the morning after a breakup. Except this morning, it was her relationship with *him* that was going to end.

The irony was not lost on her, no matter how painful the realization was.

DYLAN FINISHED WHISKING the pancake batter, then

added a generous scoop of mini chocolate chips and stirred those in, too. After weeks apart, the normalcy of this simple routine with Serena relieved him. Made him feel like everything was getting back to the way it was supposed to be between them, even if that meant navigating their way through this new change in their relationship and figuring out how to make it all work.

All he cared about was that he had Serena back. That she was his again, and Coffee Bean Guy would be a thing of the past.

Smiling at the thought, he set the bowl back down on the counter and turned around to head back to Serena's bedroom to wake her up with the caress of his hands along her body, the wet heat of his mouth drifting down her stomach, and the stroke of his tongue between her thighs before they ate breakfast, but came up short when he found her standing at the entrance to the kitchen, wearing way too many clothes. In fact, he'd left his shirt in the bedroom and he was surprised she wasn't wearing it like she normally would.

"Hey, you," he murmured, the sight of her making him smile as he approached her with seduction in mind. "I was just going to wake you up with a nice good-morning orgasm before I made you your favorite breakfast, but we can improvise here in the kitchen."

When he reached her, she put a hand up against

his chest and shook her head much too adamantly. "No."

A sinking feeling swirled in his stomach, and he tried not to let it completely inundate him with misgivings. But something wasn't right. Last night, there had been no reservations or doubts between them. Serena had been so open and sensual with him, so uninhibited and unreserved, holding back nothing.

This morning, that woman was nowhere to be seen. Instead, in her place was someone determined to keep him at arm's length, physically and emotionally. And the anguish he saw shimmering in her eyes didn't bode well for him at all.

"Last night was a mistake," she said, the words leaving her in a rush, as if she was afraid she'd lose the nerve if she didn't get it right out into the open. "I never should have let it happen. I had a moment of weakness and I'm sorry."

Flashbacks of that morning in Vegas with Serena slapped him in the face with the hurt and rejection he'd inflicted upon her. *It was a mistake.* They were the same exact words he'd said to her, and being on the receiving end of them was like a jolt to his entire system. For him, he'd gone into last night with his eyes wide open because he wanted her so damn much . . . and she clearly regretted what had happened.

"How can you call five screaming orgasms a mistake?" he asked, knowing he probably sounded like a jerk, but unable to help himself from pointing out how good they'd been together.

She slowly lowered her hand from his chest, her eyes sad as they met and held his. "I'm not going to deny that we're great together physically, but this thing we're doing? It's not healthy for either one of us, and it's not going to go anywhere because you're one hundred percent right about something you've said to me at least a dozen times over the past few years. I *do* deserve better. I deserve a guy who is going to be all in, every day. Who is going to love me the way I deserve to be loved. Deeply and unconditionally so I never have to wonder if I'm enough. And I deserve to be more than just a best friend with benefits."

He sucked in a harsh breath at that last part. "Jesus, Serena. You're so much more than a hookup!"

She shook her head in disagreement. "More than a hookup, but clearly not enough to commit yourself to."

It wasn't a question, but rather a statement based on the patterns of his relationships, or lack thereof, throughout his adult life. Which usually resulted with whoever he was dating at the time leaving him because he couldn't give them all of himself. Just as Serena had said.

She swallowed hard, a wealth of vulnerable emotions passing across her features. "I think it's probably best if we . . . go our separate ways."

Fuck. He jammed his fingers through his hair, trying to keep his shit together. "So, you're ending a lifetime friendship, just like that?" His voice was high-pitched and incredulous.

"I can't do it any other way, Dylan," she said, crossing her arms over her chest. "We can't go back to the way things were before Vegas because too much has changed, and we can't keep jumping into bed together because having sex with you, for me, means love. And you . . . well, you've taken a traumatic incident in your past with your parents and decided to let it warp your version of what love is. The two will never mesh and it makes no sense to try and force what we once were, because now it hurts too much to be with you and I need more than you're willing to give."

She didn't give him a chance to reply before she turned and walked back out of the kitchen to her bedroom, and what the hell was wrong with him that he just let her go? He was so torn and conflicted after everything she'd just said, and he couldn't disagree that his parents' divorce had messed him up and skewed his perception of what love really was.

The last thing he'd ever want to do was hurt Serena, and he knew he couldn't keep jerking her emotions around. But he had no idea what to say or do to make everything right again. All he knew was that he had to get his head on straight and figure it out, but that was so much easier said than done when he'd never been in a position where he had to open himself up and be vulnerable with a woman. Hell, he'd never wanted to before.

And now that he did, he didn't know how. And the possibility that he'd never be able to be everything Serena needed scared the shit out of him and kept him rooted in place.

SERENA STAYED LATE after school ended to work on the next week's lesson plan for her students, and also because she hated going home to her empty, lonely apartment where she was reminded of Dylan and their breakup almost a week ago. She still couldn't believe they'd severed their lifelong friendship, and the thought still made her eyes sting and her throat tighten with stupid emotional tears.

She was trying hard to move on with her life, and it was a difficult, day-to-day process without having her best friend around to call and talk to, or watch Hallmark movies with. It just wasn't the same without Dylan's funny, cheesy commentary during the shows that always made her laugh. But now, when she watched the movies by herself, she couldn't help but wonder if she'd ever get her own happily ever after. One thing was certain—she wasn't going to settle for anything less than the kind of unconditional love those heroines in the movie ended up with.

The same morning she'd ended things with Dylan, she'd called Coffee Bean Guy (the nickname actually amused her now) and did the same with him, because she'd known that if she could sleep with Dylan while dating Grant, then he wasn't the guy for her, no matter how great of a catch he was. She hadn't wanted to lead Grant on, or hurt him, because he *was* a nice guy. Just not for her. Right now, and for the foreseeable future, she was taking a break from men and dating.

She walked through the classroom and placed a worksheet on each child's desk for them to start on when they sat down Monday morning. The sound of someone opening the closed door made Serena glance up. She gave Chelsea a smile as she strolled inside.

"Hey there," Serena said, glancing at the clock on the wall and seeing it was after four in the afternoon. "Thought you'd be gone for the day by now."

"I was in the teachers' lounge talking with Callie," she said of the school's full-time nurse, and a mutual friend. "We were wondering if you were busy on Saturday."

"No, I do *not* want to go on another blind date,"

Serena replied immediately, unable to forget the last time Chelsea had set her up, and how things had ended with Ashton at Leo and Peyton's wedding. Besides, she was far from ready to move on from Dylan, even knowing there was no future with him.

Chelsea laughed. "Don't worry, I'm totally respecting your current vow of celibacy."

That was Chelsea's way of interpreting the break Serena was taking from dating any new guys, and she couldn't help but roll her eyes. She just didn't understand how some women could casually have sex with a random guy and move on, as Chelsea had with Eric. Serena just wasn't built that way. Maybe if she was, things would have ended differently between her and Dylan, or not at all and they'd both be enjoying a whole lot of hot, phenomenal sex.

She shook that thought from her head, because it was a moot point. Serena was not, and never would be, some guy's booty call. "Okay, what's happening on Saturday?" she asked curiously.

"It's an all-girl lunch down at Seaport Village with cocktails," Chelsea said with a grin. "No men allowed. I swear." She made a little cross over her heart with her index finger.

Serena bit her bottom lip as she remembered the email invite she'd received a few days ago from Aiden's wife, Daisy, announcing an engagement celebration for Dylan's mom, Grace, and her beau, Charles, that upcoming Saturday afternoon. Serena was genuinely happy for the two of them, but she hadn't responded yet because she knew it would mean facing Dylan and she wasn't sure she was ready for that just yet.

But Grace had always been like a mom to her, more than her own mother had ever been, and she knew that she needed to stop by and congratulate the couple, despite not seeing or talking to Dylan for the past week. She also enjoyed Daisy and Peyton's company, and cuddles from baby Isabella would just be a bonus. The thought made her smile.

She glanced back at Chelsea as she finished passing out the worksheets. "That sounds like fun, but I actually have something I need to do that day. Maybe next time?"

Chelsea's gaze softened perceptively. "Sure, as long as you swear you're doing okay after the whole Dylan thing?"

Serena appreciated her friend's concern, and was grateful that she'd had a friend to confide in. "I'm good." Which was true. She was hanging in there, and maybe one day soon she'd upgrade that status to great. Or not.

"Okay. But if you change your mind, just let me know and you can join us," Chelsea said, then added with a wink, "We can man bash if that would make you feel any better."

Serena laughed. "No thanks, but you and Callie have a good time."

"We will," she replied as she sauntered out the door.

Chapter Eleven

DYLAN FELT LIKE an addict who'd gone too long without a hit, with Serena as his drug of choice, and the withdrawals were kicking his ass and making every day without her a living hell. With every person who came through his mother's front door for the casual engagement celebration being held in her and Charles' honor, Dylan felt more and more anxious and on edge, knowing that at some point, it was going to be Serena who walked in.

The past week had been one of the most painful he'd ever endured, and the reason centered all around a beautiful blue-eyed blonde who'd turned his life upside down and inside out by walking out of his life. Even if he did agree that she was better off without him and his fucking mixed signals.

Needing a drink, he left the living room, where Charles and Grace were talking to a few of their friends who'd stopped by, and walked into the kitchen, where most of the family was hanging out. Not in the mood for idle chitchat and not caring for the intent way Leo had been eyeing him since he'd arrived, Dylan grabbed a bottled beer from the refrigerator, popped the top, then leaned against the counter. As he drank the cold brew, he watched his brothers interact with their significant others, feeling, for the first time, like the odd man out.

Both Leo and Aiden had found amazing women, who they'd married and were building their lives with. They had someone to come home to every night, someone to share their day with, and to wake up to every morning. Dylan always swore he didn't want or need any of those things, that he was just fine being on his own . . . except he was coming to realize that he'd never been completely alone. No, he'd always had Serena around to share all those things with. She'd *always* been there for him, through thick and thin . . . and now she wasn't.

As he watched his brothers interact with their wives, it was clear that those women were now *their* bests friends. The one person who was their every-thing. They shared inside jokes, finished each other's sentences, and indulged in affectionate glances and knowing smiles. Dylan had only had that kind of bond with one woman in his entire life—Serena. And he only wanted those intimate moments with her, and the thought of never having that with Serena ever again sliced through him like a knife.

And then he heard her voice drifting in from the living room and everything inside him crashed in a jumble of emotions. Anxiety. Anticipation. Hope. And so many fucking doubts he still hadn't figured a way to sort them all out.

A few moments later, she entered the kitchen, greeting everyone standing around the wooden island with hellos and a cheerful, radiant smile that made her eyes sparkle, especially when she cooed at Isabella. When she finally spotted him standing off to the side by himself, for the briefest, sweetest moment, he caught that genuinely candid happiness she'd always reserved just for him before she tensed and her expression fell into a polite, contained mask of civility.

She gave him an obligatory nod. "Dylan."

"Serena," he acknowledged, hating the gruff tone of his voice, the ache settling in his chest, and the mile-wide distance stretching between them when they were really only a few feet apart.

And that's all he got, just a cordial acknowledgement before she turned back to Daisy to take Baby Isabella into her arms to talk and play with her while chatting with the other two women.

The hours seemed to drag on for Dylan. He visited with the family friends who came by, and ate the catered lunch his mother had provided for everyone.

His gaze was constantly on Serena, and even a few times he'd caught *her* looking at *him* with what he'd swear was longing, but just when he thought about approaching her, she turned away again, and that stopped him cold every damn time.

"What's going on between you and Serena?" Leo asked when Dylan had retreated to the back porch for fresh air, and also so he didn't have to subject himself to seeing Serena or hearing her laugh at something someone else said.

Leaning against the railing enclosing the deck, Dylan kept his gaze averted to the landscaped backyard so he didn't have to meet his brother's too perceptive gaze. It was annoying enough that he'd felt that stare on him for most of the afternoon.

"Nothing is going on," he said, keeping his tone neutral. "Everything is fine."

Leo snickered sarcastically. "Oh, is that why the tension between the two of you is nearly tangible and you won't get within touching or speaking distance of one another? Not to mention the way you keep looking at her like you're a love-sick puppy?"

Jesus, he couldn't even deny the unflattering comparison. "Don't be a dick," he muttered irritably.

"Then don't be a fucking idiot," his brother shot back, which finally made Dylan turn his head to look at Leo. "Clearly, something major happened, because

I've never seen you two avoid each other like the plague. Serena has always worn her heart on her sleeve when it comes to you, but today, she looks like a woman who's had that same heart trampled all over. It's awkward as fuck and I want to know what you did to drive her away."

Dylan huffed out a breath and dragged his fingers through his hair. "I didn't drive her away," he said, his tone gruff. "She walked away. It was her decision, not mine." But in truth, he'd never given her a reason to stay. He could have most likely stopped her with the right words, but emotional verbiage was not his forte.

"Does this have anything to do with the night the two of you spent together in Vegas?"

Dylan's brows shot up in surprise. "How do you know about that?"

"Eric is my business partner. I work with him every single day," Leo said, outing the other man. "Not only did he tell me that the two of you slept together, he also mentioned that you dragged him to trivia night and that you had the equivalent of a pissing match with her date."

Dylan inwardly winced, knowing that hadn't been one of his finer moments.

"So, what are you going to do about this situation with Serena?" Leo pressed. "Because you can't let it go on like this."

No shit, he thought in annoyance. "Did I *ask* for your opinion on the matter?" he snapped.

"No, you didn't ask, but I'm going to give it to you anyway," his brother replied, completely unfazed by Dylan's grumpy attitude. "When are you finally going to pull your head out of your ass and realize that Serena belongs to you and the two of you were meant for one another?"

"She doesn't belong to me," he argued, glancing away again.

His brother smacked him alongside the back of his head with a loud *thump*, and not gently. The slap was hard enough that Dylan glared at Leo, a little pissed off. "What the fuck was that for?"

"To get your goddamn attention," Leo stated impatiently. "And because I want you to listen to me and let this sink into your thick, nerdy brain before you really lose the best thing in your life. Have you ever wondered, *really* wondered, why Serena hasn't already settled down with someone?"

Dylan smirked. The answer to that question was an easy one. "Because all the guys she's dated have been dicks or assholes?"

"Okay, yeah, there have been a few of those," Leo agreed with a laugh. "But I think there has always been a bigger reason that no man has ever been good enough, even the really suitable ones she's come across. Has it ever occurred to you that maybe those guys don't measure up to Serena's expectations because they aren't *you*?"

"The thing is, I *don't* measure up," Dylan replied, rolling his rigid shoulders. "She's a woman who wants the whole entire fairy tale and happily-ever-after, and when have I ever been able to give that to any woman? Never, because it's always been easier for me to let the relationship end." Except for Serena, who, until now, had always been a constant in his life. "What if I try a real relationship with Serena and end up fucking it all up or hurting her in the long run?" It was thoughts like that that paralyzed him with fear.

"You've already done that, asshole." Leo studied him seriously. "Look, there are no guarantees for the long run, Dylan, and there are going to be times that you screw up. And I get that giving someone all of your heart is not an easy thing to do, but have you looked around at our family lately?" Leo asked, glancing back inside the glass slider to the kitchen and the people they loved most mingling there. "You've got Aiden, who swore he'd never settle down, and now he's married with a kid and already talking about having more. And if I can get dumped at the altar on my wedding day and still find the true love of my life with Peyton, then there's hope for you, too. And then there's Mom, who's been through hell with Dad and her cancer scare, but has found a guy who treats her like a queen and is going to marry her and give her everything she deserves. She's found love again, and it's bigger and stronger than it ever was with Dad. Trust me when I tell you that you already love Serena, that she's your forever girl. She always has been."

"And what happens if I can't give her what she needs?" he asked, not fully convinced because he wanted what was best for Serena. Forget about himself.

"For a guy who's so intelligent, you're incredibly stupid about some things," Leo said with humor. "Dylan, *you* are what she needs. And you need her. You always have."

Dylan couldn't refute that, but it was difficult to squash the doubts that lingered.

"I want you to imagine something," Leo said after a few quiet minutes had passed. "Imagine watching Serena walking down the aisle at her wedding . . . to another man. How does that make you feel?"

Like he wanted to puke. "Fine," he forced out. "I'd feel fine."

"And when that other guy puts a ring on her finger and she commits the rest of her life to him, until death do they part, how does *that* make you feel?"

Absolutely dead inside. "I'll be happy for her. It's what she deserves." He forced the words out, because

153

wasn't that what he'd been telling himself all this time?

"Bullshit," his brother muttered. "And what about what you deserve?" Leo pushed on. "Don't you deserve a woman who makes you happy the way Serena does?"

Dylan shook his head and rubbed his hand down his face. "I don't know what I deserve anymore. I just know I can't keep hurting Serena, but not having her in my life is killing me, too."

"Then put a goddamn ring on her finger already," his brother said, clapping him on the back. "Trust me, you're all she needs, but she needs *all* of you, not just a half-assed version of yourself that's scared to put your heart on the line for her."

Leo's words stayed with Dylan for the rest of the afternoon, rolling around in his head and giving him the time he needed to build up the courage to take that leap of faith. As the party finally came to an end and everyone was gone but immediate family, his mother, Grace, came into the kitchen, where everyone was gathered, along with Charles, and placed an old-style photo album on the island counter.

"What a day," his mother said, all smiles and beaming radiantly.

"We're all so happy for both of you," Peyton said, giving Grace a warm hug. "You two are clearly meant for one another."

"I do have to say that love has been so much sweeter the second time around," Grace said with a content sigh as she stared into Charles' eyes. "I can't wait to marry this man of mine."

Charles drew her close and placed an affectionate kiss on her temple. "The honor will be all mine, sweetheart."

Aiden groaned. "Okay, you two, if you don't quit, we're going to have to insist you get a room."

A bright pink blush stained Dylan's mother's cheeks, and she turned back to the photo album she'd brought into the kitchen. "I came across something while I was going through old boxes that brought back some fun memories and made me smile. Dylan and Serena, come here. I want to show you this."

Serena reluctantly moved next to Grace, and Dylan stood next to Serena, close enough that he could inhale the floral scent of her shampoo and feel the warmth of her body next to his. His fingers itched to touch, but he didn't dare give in to the temptation.

"This is a scrapbook I made of the two of you growing up," Grace said, flipping the book open to the first page, which showed pictures of Dylan and Serena as toddlers playing in a plastic pool together, splashing each other and having fun.

He caught Serena's melancholy smile, while Daisy and Peyton crowded around to get a better look and *awww*'d in unison. His mother turned the page, revealing images of them a bit older, around four, eating cupcakes Grace had made and smearing frosting in each other's face. Everyone laughed and made jokes but Serena, who seemed to be trying very hard not to show her emotions.

More pictures as they grew up together . . . with Serena all frilly in a princess outfit that his mother had made for her to wear for Halloween, and him in a Disney prince costume, which he did not look happy about getting stuck with—and his brothers were currently teasing him about. He clearly remembered wanting to be a superhero villain instead, but the sweet, adoring expression captured on Serena's face as she looked at him was pure infatuation, and her crush on him had started around then, which Dylan had been oblivious to at the time.

His mother had captured a photo of the two of them lying in the grass in Dylan's backyard, their heads close together as they stared up at the clouds and pointed out all the different shapes and images they'd found—with him holding her hand as if she'd belonged to him even then. More fun, casual pictures through middle school, with Dylan's arm slung over her shoulder and those pretty blue eyes once again gazing up at him as if he'd hung the moon and stars for her.

Yes, it was clear for everyone in the room to see that Serena had worn her heart on her sleeve for him. And he'd been a clueless kid.

The album ended just as high school began, and that significance wasn't lost on Dylan, because that's when his feelings for Serena started to change, when he'd become aware of her as more than just his best pal, and desire and teenage lust had him noticing the new, shapely curves of her body. When the urge to kiss her became too unbearable, he'd focused on other girls instead. He'd deliberately spent less time with Serena and firmly kept her in the friend zone because of his fear of losing her.

Now, he realized he'd fallen in love with her back then, and years later, those feelings had only grown stronger and deeper, despite his attempts to keep them tucked away, always to protect Serena from himself. But the truth was, nobody could ever compare to her, and nobody ever would.

His mother closed the book and pushed it toward Serena. "I thought you might like to keep this, since it's pictures of you and Dylan."

Serena bit her bottom lip, which quivered slightly, and shook her head. "I appreciate the gesture. I really do. But I think Dylan should take it," she said, her voice husky, as if she were holding back tears. But then she exhaled a deep breath and pasted on a smile.

"It's been a wonderful party, but it's getting late and I really should go."

Dylan recognized her abrupt departure for what it was—an excuse to put distance between them, to lessen the pain she was so obviously feeling. It was a Saturday evening and it wasn't as though she had to work the next day. He watched as she made the rounds, saying goodbye and hugging each person in the family . . . except him. Hell, she wouldn't even look his way, and when she walked out of the kitchen and down the hall to the guest room, where the girls had left their purses, his brother Leo shot him a look that said, *It's now or never.*

It was definitely *now.* With everyone staring expectantly at him, clearly waiting to see what his next move would be, he followed the direction that Serena had just taken.

Chapter Twelve

SERENA HEARD THE sound of soft, padded footsteps into the guest room, and certain it was either Peyton or Daisy checking up on her, she quickly dashed away the tears that had slipped from the corners of her eyes after that too emotional trip down memory lane, which only reminded her of what she would never have with Dylan. The boy she'd grown up with, the teenager she'd had a crush on, and the man she'd fallen in love with.

She turned around, startled to find Dylan standing there instead. She didn't say a word, but as he closed the distance between them, her heart threatened to beat right out of her chest.

"Serena," he said, so softly, so tenderly that it threw her more off-kilter than she already was. And when he picked up her hand and clasped his warm ones around it, her first reaction was to try and pull it back.

He held it tighter, not letting her escape. "Please,

just listen to me, okay?"

She didn't say anything, mostly because her throat felt too tight, but figured since she wasn't walking away from him, that ought to be enough of an answer for him. She was here. She'd listen. But she wasn't sure there was anything left to say.

He swallowed hard, his Adam's apple bobbing nervously. "I handled things very poorly that morning at your place, and I'm so sorry. I never should have let you walk away from me. I never should have left without telling you how I feel."

For a moment, she held her breath, wondering if he'd finally say the words she desperately longed to hear him say.

"I care about you so much," he said, his voice as sincere as the look in his eyes. "We're good together, and you know me better than anyone else. You're my person, and I want you, and only you."

There was no *I love you* to be found anywhere in that sentence. The hope that had blossomed in Serena's chest wilted. The man standing in front of her was speaking logically and practically, his words coming from that pragmatic brain of his, and not his heart, where it mattered the most. After everything they'd been through, she needed more than just the logistics of why they belonged together. She wanted, needed the emotional, vulnerable component of it, too.

She shook her head sadly and withdrew her hand from his. "It's not enough, Dylan. I deserve better. I deserve *more*."

His brows creased in confusion, as if she were speaking in Greek back to him. In any other situation, she would have thought his reaction was adorably geeky, but in this case, when it came to winning her heart and winning *her*, she refused to spell out what she needed to hear from him, because hand-feeding him the words was too easy. It was something he had to figure out on his own, and he would, eventually, if he thought she was worth fighting for.

"More?" He echoed the word back to her, his expression perplexed. "What kind of more?"

God, he was so obtuse sometimes, and she gave him his one and only clue. "I want the fairy tale, Dylan."

SHE WANTED THE fairy tale. Serena's final statement to him before leaving Dylan standing alone in his mother's guest bedroom was still rolling through his brain by the time he got home that same night. After she was gone, he'd walked back to the kitchen in a stupor, where Leo, who obviously knew why he'd gone after Serena, looked at him and immediately asked, "What did she say?"

"That she wanted the fairy tale," he said, dumbfounded by what had just happened. He'd gone into the room believing he was going to win the girl, and instead he'd fallen flat on his face with a big ol' *whomp-whomp*.

Leo and Aiden had shared a laugh, and he'd watched Daisy and Peyton exchange an amused look. Even Isabella had blown a raspberry at him. The fact that he was left in the dark about Serena's request annoyed the hell out of him.

He'd jammed his hands on his hips indignantly. "Anyone care to share what that means?"

"Nah," Aiden had said before anyone else could provide the answer, his voice brimming with merriment. "I think it'll be more fun, and way more meaningful, for you to figure it out on your own."

"Asshole," he'd muttered.

And now, he was at home by himself, sitting on his couch and absently flipping through the channels on his TV while mulling over what kind of fairy tale Serena was referring to. The only ones he knew of were in Disney movies. Pure fiction and not based in reality.

He came across the Hallmark Channel and stopped to watch the movie that was playing, wishing Serena was there with him because it was more fun viewing it with her than alone. Before long, he was sucked into the over-the-top, corny romance as the same old basic plot played out between the guy and the girl. He knew the story line by heart. They met and sparks flew. Usually there was some kind of opposition between the characters that caused a conflict to keep them separated. Then the big black moment, where the two of them were torn apart by their differences and all seemed lost.

But it was the part where they came to the realization that they just couldn't live without one another that riveted Dylan, because it led into the cheesiest grand gesture from the guy that ultimately won the woman's heart and made her swoon, along with a declaration of unending love.

Realization finally dawned. *That* was the fucking fairy tale that Serena was talking about. The words *I love you* that left no doubt in the woman's mind that the guy was deeply, madly in love with her. Which was exactly how he felt about Serena . . . but he'd never told her.

Jesus Christ, it was that simple, but for a logic-minded guy, the notion had eluded him. But for a sentimental woman like Serena who was waiting to find her Prince Charming to sweep her off her feet, those heartfelt words meant everything.

And now that he knew what she wanted, what she needed, he was going to give Serena the fairy tale she'd waited her whole life for, and the one she deserved.

✦   ✦   ✦

WHEN SERENA'S DOORBELL rang late Sunday afternoon, her first thought was that it was Dylan. Instead, when she peered through the peephole, she saw an older man dressed in a black suit that looked like a uniform. Confused, she cracked the door open so she could look at the gentleman, who greeted her with a smile.

"Can I help you?" she asked, certain he was at the wrong door.

"Are you Serena Fields?" he asked politely.

"Yes." Now she was even more perplexed.

"My name is Duke Frasier," he said, introducing himself as he lifted a shiny, gray Nordstrom's box, topped with a big bow, toward her. There was also an envelope with her name on it. "This package is for you, from Dylan Stone."

Surprise lit through her. "Oh." She accepted the package, unable to guess what might be inside. "Thank you."

Duke nodded. "There's a note in the envelope. I'll wait right here while you read it and follow the instructions inside." He stepped away from the door and assumed a professional stance.

After closing the door, she headed into the kitchen

and set the box on the counter. She opened the envelope first and read the message inside. *Serena, please change into this outfit and leave with Duke. He will take you where you need to be. I promise you won't regret it. Dylan.*

She wrinkled her nose in surprise and confusion. It was all so cryptic, considering she hadn't seen or heard from him since last night at his mother's. But she was willing to follow his request, because she still loved him and wanted to hold on to hope.

Lifting the lid on the box, she moved the tissue paper aside and gasped at what she found inside. A gorgeous dress in a violet hue, with a fitted bodice and a flowy chiffon skirt. There was also a pair of bone-colored heels to go with it. The outfit was far more modest than the one she'd worn in Vegas, but much more her style. She couldn't imagine that he'd picked it out himself, but in this case, she was okay going with *it was the thought that counted.*

She changed, and after a quick look in the mirror, she decided to put on a light layer of makeup and leave her hair down and wavy, just the way she knew Dylan liked it best. Twenty minutes later, she met Duke outside, and he led the way out to a limousine parked at the curb and opened the back door for her. She slid onto the soft, supple leather seat and saw that there was already a flute of champagne waiting for her in the glass holder and an open box of Godiva with her favorite chocolates tucked inside.

"We'll arrive at our destination in about fifteen minutes," Duke said, then enclosed her in the back, while he got behind the wheel and started to drive.

Feeling decadently spoiled, she drank her champagne and nibbled on the rich candy, trying to figure out, based on their route, where Duke was taking her. It didn't take her long to realize that he was heading to Dylan's house, and when they arrived and she stepped out of the limo, there was a trail of red rose petals all the way up the pathway to the front door.

She started to feel giddy, from the champagne and this romantic gesture that was straight out of one of her Hallmark movies. Anticipation had her following the deep red blooms, and even when she walked inside the house, the trail continued all the way to Dylan's master bedroom. The door was closed, but she could hear soft music playing inside.

Her heart beat so fast it felt as though it had wings. Swallowing nervously, she knocked lightly, and when Dylan's voice beckoned her to come in, she followed his order. A shocked gasp escaped her as she took in the transformation of his bedroom. There were white twinkle lights everywhere. Hundreds of them sparkling like a dreamy, romantic wonderland. More flowers were scattered on the floor, and the bed had been turned down, where a heart had been formed with roses.

But it was the gorgeous man standing there wearing a dark suit—which was something Dylan only did on formal occasions—that stole her breath completely. He was grinning, but it was the wealth of emotion shining in his eyes that had her walking toward him, praying that this huge grand gesture came with the most important declaration of all. Because without it, all this meant nothing.

He held his hand out toward her. "Dance with me?" he asked, surprising her.

"Yes." She let him draw her into his arms and against the warmth of his body, where she fit against him perfectly.

Curling her arm around his neck, she glanced up at him, into the eyes that looked at her with pure, undiluted adoration. "This is all too much," she whispered. But it wasn't. Not after all he'd put her through.

"Not for you." He gently kissed her temple. "I wanted to give you your fairy tale, Serena. All of it."

The sweetness of it made her melt inside, even as a part of her remained guarded as she waited to see where all this would lead. "It's impressive. I'm going to assume you had help?"

"Maybe a little." He continued dancing with her, the hand around her waist tightening possessively. "Everything was my idea, but Peyton and Daisy were more than happy to pull it together while I ran a few errands for tonight."

She felt his chest rise and fall as he inhaled and exhaled a deep breath, his feet coming to a stop so they were no longer moving. He reached out and gently caressed her cheek.

"There's something I need to say to you," he said huskily, his eyes darkening with emotion. "I love you, Serena, and that's not something I figured out just recently. It's something I've known since high school, but I was too afraid to jeopardize our friendship. There has been no other woman that I've ever loved. Only you."

She laughed softly, joyfully, the relief in her chest immense. "You figured it out." She couldn't stop the huge smile on her face.

He sighed, but he was grinning. "I'm a little slow and hardheaded sometimes, but I swear I can be trained with the right incentive," he teased.

"I love you, Dylan Stone," she said, needing him to hear those words from her, too. "So much."

"I know. I've always known, but hearing the words out loud is something I'll never get tired of." His hand traveled slowly, sensually, down her back. "I want you to have the future you deserve. The husband, the marriage, the family, and all the babies you were meant to have. I always wanted that for you. But I realized something . . ."

She blinked back the happy tears filling her eyes, but her heart was beginning to soar at the realization that all her dreams were gradually coming true. "What's that?"

"I'm a selfish man when it comes to you," he said, a possessive tone to his voice. "You're mine, and I want to be the man who gives you all those things."

She smiled. "There is no other man I'd ever want to have those things with."

Relief passed across his handsome features, followed by a hint of nerves. "Okay, since that's settled, then there is just one more thing left to do."

She blinked curiously at him. "You've already done so much."

"There's just one more thing missing from this cheesy Hallmark-style grand gesture," he joked, as he released her to reach into the front pocket of his pants.

In the next few seconds, he was down on one knee before her, popping open the lid on a small black velvet box that revealed a stunning engagement ring. "Serena Fields, you are the love of my life. Will you marry me?"

She couldn't deny the jolt of shock that ran through her because he'd come so far so fast, but she didn't hesitate with her answer, because she'd waited a lifetime to say the words to him. "Yes, yes, I'll marry you."

He slipped the ring onto her finger, which was a perfect fit, then stood back up and kissed her—hot and deep and packed with so much feeling she never wanted it to end. They melted together with all the passion and longing they'd both been holding back, and when he started unzipping her dress, she took that as her cue to help him out of his clothes, too.

When they were completely naked—except for the gorgeous ring on her finger—he pushed her down onto the bed, aligned their bodies, and eased deep, deep inside her. His hands came up to cradle her face, and she opened her eyes to look into his, marveling at the fact that she was going to marry her best friend.

"You belong to me," he said, leaving no doubt in her mind that it was true.

"Yes," she whispered, and she wouldn't want it any other way.

Epilogue

SERENA WOKE UP a few hours later, alone in Dylan's bed, the twinkling lights still on, which she secretly loved because it was so romantic. Actually, she'd loved everything about Dylan's grand gesture, and especially the part where he'd professed his love. Really, deep down inside, she was just a simple girl and it didn't take much to make her happy.

Dylan made her happy. So very happy, she thought with a smile.

Curious to know where he'd gone when it wasn't even midnight, she got out of bed, pulled one of his T-shirts from his dresser drawer, and slipped it on. She'd missed being able to do that, she thought. Then she went in search of her fiancé. She grinned blissfully. Ahhh, the sound of *that* made her really happy, too.

She found him in his office down the hall, sitting at his desk with his laptop open, his fingers typing and his mouth curved in a mischievous grin. She came up behind him, slid her hands around to his chest, and placed a warm kiss on his cheek, then glanced at the computer and saw the beta version of the Boyfriend Experience app open on the screen.

"What are you doing in here?" she chided softly. "If you're working, shut it down and come back to bed."

"Not working," he murmured, as he continued entering information into a text box. "I'm creating a profile for Eric on the Boyfriend Experience app."

"Oh." She looked closer and saw that Dylan had already uploaded a recent photo of Eric, too. "He agreed to be one of the beta testers?"

"No, not really," Dylan said with a light laugh. He reached for her and pulled her across his lap, so she was sitting on his thighs. "I'm *volunteering* him for the job."

Her eyes widened. "Are you sure he's going to be okay with that?"

"I'm positive he's not," Dylan replied with a chuckle. "But what's the fun of him knowing he's got a profile on the app ahead of time? He deserves this after all the shit he gave me at trivia night. It's just a little friendly payback."

She bit her bottom lip, though the thought of some woman tying Eric up in knots appealed to her more than it should. "I can't wait to see what happens."

"We'll find out soon enough. Beta testing begins next week."

If you enjoyed Dylan and Serena's story, please consider leaving an honest review for **TALL, DARK & TEMPTING** at your e-tailer. It only takes a moment and is very helpful in spreading the word to other readers. Thank you!

UP NEXT FROM ERIKA WILDE & CARLY PHILLIPS!

Curious to read Eric Miller's story from TALL, DARK & TEMPTING? Don't miss his book, TO-TAL PACKAGE, the first book in our Boyfriend Experience series!

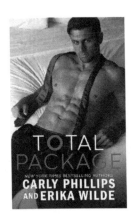

Looking for a temporary guy for a special occasion or event? Then the Boyfriend Experience app is for you!

Eric Miller isn't thrilled when a friend signs him up for The Boyfriend Experience app behind his back. It's not like he has a problem getting women on his own. But when he gets a notification that someone is in need of his . . . services, he's intrigued enough to check out her profile and can't resist the sexy, sassy little blonde who only wants him as a decoy for her family reunion.

Evie Bennett needs a boyfriend, stat. Someone who is the total package and can accompany her to her family reunion so she doesn't have to hear all about how she needs to settle down like the rest of her cousins have. She's perfectly happy being an independent woman, but what's a girl to do when The Boyfriend Experience starts to feel like the real deal?

Order **TOTAL PACKAGE** today!

To stay up to date on Erika Wilde's latest releases, please sign-up for her newsletter here:

erikawilde.com/subscribe

Other Books in the
Tall, Dark & Sexy Series

Book 1: Tall, Dark & Charming (Aiden and Daisy)
Book 2: Tall, Dark & Irresistible (Leo and Peyton)
Book 3: Tall, Dark & Tempting (Dylan and Serena)

To learn more about The Marriage Diaries and interact with the series and characters, please like my Erika Wilde Author Facebook Fan Page at:

www.facebook.com/groups/erikawildesfanclub

To learn more about Erika Wilde and her upcoming releases, you can visit her at the following places on the web:

Website:
erikawilde.com

Facebook:
facebook.com/groups/erikawildesfanclub

Twitter:
twitter.com/erikawilde1

Goodreads:
goodreads.com/erikawildeauthor